I0546540

Sister's Keeper

Aria Daze

Daze Dream Publications

CONTENTS

CONTENT WARNINGS!

B efore you dive in, please check out these handy content warnings. Reading should be enjoyable, and some of the topics covered in this book may not be for you. Your mental health matters.

This book will definitely include the following:

- Penetrative sex

- Homosexual activities

- Oral sex

- Death of a parent/loved one.

- Anxiety

- Alcohol consumption

- Anal play

- Foul language

This book also features black people who utilize Ebonics in their speech. It's not country, improper, or ghetto, and I would not like to see any emails about it. Please feel free to email me about other things though, such as the Santa Roleplay. As always, if any of these topics sound unpleasant to you, please do not continue onward, dear reader. I have other things in my catalog that may be a better fit. **This book is not suitable for readers under the age of 18!**

Author's Note

Hey Daze Dreamers! So as some of you may know, I'm gay. Like rainbow spinner, nipple pasty, gay. While being gay isn't my entire personality, it does play a significant role in what I decide to write and how I perceive the world around me. I'm pansexual, which simply means I'm not to hung up on pesky things like gender assignment, or genitals. I like pretty people with big booties, period. Diversity in romance is my life's mission, whether it's common body diversity such as weight, height, or more nuanced things such as limb differences, disabilities, or in this particular case, girls with dicks. Jaima, one of the lesbians in this story, is a non-op trans woman. Her penis doesn't make her gender identity any less valid, so please respect her as well as the beautiful, real-life Black trans women she is modeled after.

Thanks,

Aria D

A REAL GOOD

Christmas

PLAYLIST

EARTHA KITT-
SANTA BABY

DONNY
HATHAWAY-
THIS
CHRISTMAS

LUTHER
VANDROSS- A
MERRY LITTLE
CHRISTMAS

VICTORIA
MONET-
CADILLAC
CHRISTMAS

STEVIE
WONDER-
WHAT
CHRISTMAS
MEANS TO ME

KIRBY- MERRY
LIKE THIS

COCO
JONES-STRING
LIGHTS

DRAM-COAL

1

GENESIS

H enny

"I'm getting married!"

I look at my mother's fanned-out left hand, where a giant ring rests on her comparably small index finger. That bad boy's gotta weigh at least five carrots, and it looks like something that royalty wears with its blindingly bright diamond and heavily encrusted halo band. That's not to say she doesn't deserve it. My mama and James have been dating for five years after meeting at a widower's support group, and I know it took a lot of work to put themselves back out there. So of course I'm excited for them.

"Congratulations!" I cheer.
"Thank you, sweetheart," my mama smiles. "And one other thing. We-"
"We want you to be a bridesmaid!" James interjects.
See, that's where things got sticky. I love them, and of

course, I want to be a part of their big day, but…

"Y'all, listen. I know this is important to you both, but my hair's purple in the back, and I'm covered in tattoos. I'm not exactly champagne tower picture material."

I'm grown. I chose to document my life in ink and I love my tattoos, I also love my hair. But I recognize that the more conservative members of the James And Arnetta Show did not. Why make it harder on myself?

"So damn what! You're family!" James exclaims. "Anybody got anything they want to say, they can bring it to me!"

I laugh and pat James' hand. I'm glad he's marrying my mama. He values family over everything, and ever since about year two, I've been the second daughter that he always wanted but never got to have.

"Ok, y'all got me. I'll be there," I concede with a sigh.

"Good, 'cause we got a dress appointment in six weeks exactly, and we've already set a date," Mama confirms.

Of course they have. Arnetta probably picked a date and venue before he even proposed.

"Lawd, when is it?" I ask, ready to block out the entire wedding week.

"December 25th" they reply simultaneously.

Wait, why does that sound familiar?

"Christmas?"

"That's the day!" James exclaims. "What better way to close out the holidays than with the love of my life?"

He raises Mama's chin and plants a sweet kiss on the end of her nose that causes her to simper. It's like watching Cupid pop muhfuckas in real time, I can practically see the stars floating in both of their eyes.

"Alright, this is cute but also gross. Send me the appointment information Ma'. I gotta get to work."

"Ok, baby," she chuckles. "Tat, tat, tat em up!"

I love her enthusiasm and support, but that phrase never gets easier to hear. Someone needs to hurry up and make that woman a grandma. It's her destiny.

"Alright, Ma. Alright, James. See y'all later," I sigh.

Jaima

"Where you at, girl?" Daddy calls.

Fuck.

I love my father, but he has the worst timing ever. I have a meeting in 10 minutes. A meeting with no less than twenty suits and high-power execs. A meeting that is crucial to my Q2 success.

"Uh, I'm in my library, Sir!" I reply, as I hurriedly flick on mascara.

I hate mascara, and I know I need to schedule an appointment with my lash tech. I also need my nails and feet done. I need lots of things if I'm being honest with myself, but I've been so focused on the project that I haven't made time for anything else. Having laser focus is not the blessing people think it is.

"Jesus, Jaima. I gotta come by your house to hear from you? If I didn't get doorbell alerts every time someone GroceryGrabbed you some food, I'd think you were dead."

"I'm sorry, Daddy," I sigh. "I've just been really busy."

"Jaima, it's been a month since I heard from you," he chides.

Stunned by his accusation, I check my calendar. There's no way it's been a month. Sure, I've been busy, but not neglectful. Right? I scroll for what feels like an eternity before I finally see his name highlighted on February 13th at 6 pm for a thirty-minute video chat. Today is March 22nd. It's been over a month.

"I'm embarrassed," I admit.

"Good," he nods. "You should be."

"We need to catch up, but I got this meeting in seven minutes, Sir. I really gotta prep for it."

"Don't mind me," Daddy waves. "I'm about to see what you made out of those lamb shanks you had delivered yesterday. Did you make mashed potatoes too?"

Of course, my dad is right back to normal after making me feel like the worst daughter on earth. He's already made plans for my leftovers and he's looking through the shelves for a book.

"Yes, but please, stay away from this section of the library," I wheeze, steering him away from my smut.

"Girl, I'm grown! I can read erotica. Go prep or whatever," he chides.

I check the time, hoping I can spare a few more seconds to keep him out of my sapphic fantasies, but alas I cannot. So I cringe as James Hines picks up a copy of A Little Kissing Between Friends, eyebrow hitched up high.

"Wonderful work, Ms. Hines. We can't wait to discuss and hopefully be back with some good news."

I finally let myself breathe. I've been on this meeting for an hour, talking for what feels like days while a room full of executives stares into my soul. It was so uncomfortable that I started borrowing jokes from James Hines himself, hoping to lighten the mood. Unfortunately, I don't have the smile to be able to effectively pass off corny jokes. So I'm glad my work can speak for itself.

"Thank you, I look forward to it!" I exclaim with far more cheer than I'm actually feeling.

When I went to school for engineering, I did so under the impression that I'd have high pay and low human contact. Unfortunately that's only true if you do the bare minimum. My workaholic ways had gotten me noticed and promoted, and now I was proposing a new security system for one of the biggest OS developers in the world. Isn't life funny?

"How'd your meeting go?" Daddy asks, cutting into a slice of key lime pie.

"I think it went well," I nod. "They said they're going to discuss and get back to me."

"Well, let me be the first to say congratulations, my dear," he smiles. "Also, where'd you get this pie?"

"Auntie Foxxy's."

"Mm, I need to go in there. I ain't been there in a long time," he sighs.

I sit next to my dad on the bench with a soft plop. I still feel horrible that this is our first interaction in a month, but he doesn't seem to be bothered by it anymore. He's happy with the pie.

"What's new, old man?" I ask, nudging him.

He scoffs, as if the curls around his temples haven't been graying for the last decade. If James Hines ain't have nothing else, he'd still have his pride.

"I'll have you know that I'm sixty-one years young."

"You're right, I'm sorry," I giggle. "But tell me what I've missed."

My daddy sat his plate on the side table and straightened his back to puff his chest out. Whatever he was about to tell me was life-changing. I've only seen him get in his serious pose one other time in my life, and that ended with me in tears.

"Daddy, you're scaring me," I admit.

His shoulders relax a little and his infamous smirk returns, easing my nerves.

"It's nothing bad, Jaime," he assures me. "You're just getting a new sister, that's all."

I nearly fell out of my seat while trying to catch my fleeing breath.

"You're having a baby at your age!?" I exclaim. "How did you even get somebody pregnant? What happened to Ms. Arnetta!?"

"What!? No one's pregnant! Arnetta and I are fine. Actually we're more than fine. We're getting married," he explains.

"Oh, shit," I gasp, calming my racing heart. "Then why'd you say I was getting a new sister?"

My father's expression fell into something akin to disappointment, and for the life of me I couldn't understand why. Until he reminded me,

"Arnetta's daughter, Hen. Remember?"

Henrietta Brighton, nicknamed Henny for short. She was outspoken, lively, and energetic. A stark contrast to the shy housecat energy I was bringing.

"Oh yeah," I nod.

"Yeah," Daddy sighs, patting my hand.

I swallow the last of my anxiety around the possibility of my Daddy having a baby at his big age and we sit in companionable silence for a few moments before he clears his throat to speak.

"Listen, pumpkin. I know you're used to it just being me and you, and I know Hen can be a handful, but I really want you to try and get to know her. This is important to me. I want us to be a family. A Christmas card, Jenga-night, holiday vacation, intertwined family."

My dad came from a tight-knit family of twelve, so his wanting to be close makes perfect sense. Honestly, it does sound nice, having people to bond with. Telling inside jokes over dinner, planning cool vacations, and whooping ass over Uno. Getting to know Henny sounds nice too. She's a certified bad bitch on top of being a celebrity tattoo artist with her own brand of whiskey. Maybe she could help me be less awkward and get out more.

"Ok, Daddy," I agree. "I'll try."

"Good!" he exclaims. "Cause the three of you have a dress appointment in six weeks."

"Six weeks!? God, y'all are moving fast. What if I had plans?"

"Well, it's a good thing you don't," he says, raining on my parade. "And I spent five years taking things slow, Jaima. I'm ready."

Really, it's been longer than that. My daddy spent seven years frozen after my mama died. It was hard watching that part of him die, and I wasn't sure if he'd ever open his heart again. So if he was ready, I was ready.

"Alright, Daddy," I smiled. "Consider me there."

2
DRESSED UP

Henny

"There's nothing like a little retail therapy to get you back together," Mama sighs.

She's so right. I had a shitty week. Two no call no shows, a cover-up from hell, and a fifteen-hour back piece, but the second we stepped into Bayside Marketplace, all those worries melted away.

"Mhm," I mumble as I scoop some icing into my twist. "We should've got two of these pretzels."

"Oh! You're worse than James. I'm trying to watch my figure!" She fusses.

"Mama, please!" I shoot back. "You're sixty-two and you have abs!"

I've never dreamed of having abs. Not even at my skinniest, well over ten years ago. My everything is soft. At 33

I've come to terms with my extra curvy body, but I can't say watching my mama strut around in bikinis doesn't make me the tiniest bit jealous. Maybe I wanna channel my inner Pam Grier somedays.

"Well everybody didn't get Grandma Nessa's booty," she sighs. "She passed all those genes right to you."

Yeah, and she conveniently left out the titties. I was just ass, hips, and belly. Trying on dresses was going to be so fun. I better not even think about bending over.

"What time is our appointment?" I ask.

"1:30," she replies. "We're just waiting on James and Jaima. They're riding together."

"Oh, Jaima's coming?" I croak.

I've only met Jaima twice, and she didn't seem interested in me either of those times. Quite the opposite, actually. She just stared at me the whole time, offering me a weak smile whenever she needed to prove she was still listening.

"Henny," Mama sighs.

"No, I mean. That's great, I love that she's involved. I just…" I trail off, wondering how much I should tell my mother considering this is her day.

My issue with Jaima is my own, and I know it's something I need to get over. Her Dad was marrying my mom. I couldn't avoid her forever.

"What Henny?" Mama urges.

"I just don't think she likes me," I admit.

I know I'm not everyone's cup of tea, I get it. I'm loud, I'm inappropriate, I like throwing my ass in a hendecagon. Jaima's all polished, prim, and professional. We couldn't be more different.

"No, Henny," Mama assures me. "Jaima's just, she's very shy. She ain't come from a big, loud, crazy family like us. It's been her and James for the longest time."

I thought back to our last family reunion. Me and my cousin Shane broke two tables with our shenanigans, my mama brought the jungle juice, and my aunt Mika was throwing cash on everything that shook or shimmied. It was a time to be had.

"You right," I sigh. "We do get wild."

"Exactly. Just give her a little time, baby. She'll grow on you."

"Alright, alright. But I'm grabbing another pretzel. I can't entertain an audience with low sugar," I laugh.

We get to Ballroom Bridals with five minutes to spare, and the second we reach the doors, I spot James and his daughter exiting her Benz. Her wavy black hair is tied in a sleek chingon, her caramel skin is glistening with gold highlight, and she's dressed in a champagne-colored linen plisse suit. She looks like a GQ model while I look like a struggling mechanic. I knew this was the wrong day to wear overalls.

"Hi!" she exclaims, bringing Mama in for a hug. "It's been so long. Congratulations!"

"Oh thank you, baby!" she chuckles, squeezing Jaima tight. "I'm so glad you could make it."

"I wouldn't miss it for the world," she smiles back before turning to me.

"Hi, Hen. I brought you something," she says, extending a little pink gift bag.

I almost don't want to reach for it. Not only is it gorgeous, it's also unreciprocated. Nobody told me we were exchanging gifts. What is this? A sister proposal?

"Oh I couldn't. I don't have anything to give you," I say, waving her off.

"Nonsense!" Jaima exclaims. "I insist. I made it specifically for you."

She made it for me? Oh fuck, now I had to take it. What kind of asshole rejects a personal gift?

"Thanks so much," I gulp, accepting the deceptively heavy bag. "And if you ever might want a tattoo, I can do that for you," I offer awkwardly.

My Mama cringes. We both knew I was floundering, but I had to offer her something. Knowing Jaima, she probably handmade jam or something. She looks like the type to handmake some jam. A real Nara Smith.

"Oh ok, thank you!" Jaima replies. "Should we head in?"

"Yep," I agree, reaching for the handle. "Let's try on some dresses."

Ballroom Bridals is massive. There are gowns hanging from every possible space, occupying artfully posed mannequins, and even neatly folded in clearance bins. I can't pass up a bargain, so I head for the clearance bins first while Jaima heads for the racks.

"What color do you want us in?" I ask Mama, as I spot a sunny yellow halter.

"White," she hums.

"What? White? Are you sure?" I ask.

"What color are you wearing?" Jaima adds.

"Yes, I'm sure. I always wanted an all white wedding. Besides, I'm technically wearing blush."

Her fingers dance over patches of pink-tinted lace and satin, all wonderful contenders for her dream dress.

"I think it'll look beautiful on you," Jaima hums as she plucks a gown from a spinning rack. "What about this one?"

The dress is stunning.

It's made of taffeta and a hint of lace, allowing for a tasteful amount of skin to peek through at her back and over the tops of her chest. The bell sleeves are also made of lace, and they dramatically flow down the fitted bodice, the ends falling just below the hips where the gown begins to flare. Me and Mama gasp at the same time when Jaima twirls it around.

"When I was about your age I wanted a dress just like that, but I was broke as a joke," Mama chuckles. "Now I have the money for it, but I may be too old."

"Nonsense!" James shouts over the partition. "My baby looks damn good in anything."

"He's right, Mama," I nod. "You should try it on at the very least."

Mama's fingertips float over the intricate patches of lace with an air of caution. Then the most wistful sigh escapes her lips.

"I'll try it on, but I'm gonna find two more I like just in case."

We all know that the other dresses are just a formality at this point, and Jaima lets a triumphant little smirk peek through her prim and polished exterior. Her proud toothy smile is both adorable and dazzling, but as soon as she realizes what she's done, she tucks it back inside her veil of mysteries. I hate to admit that I feel a great

personal loss when she does. Who is Jaima really?
"Let's try on some dresses, ladies!" she claps, bringing me
back to reality.
A reality without full, toothy grins.

"I don't like it."
The three of us express our disappointment simultaneously. The dress mama has on is fine, but it's not her.
It's too matronly. Clean straight lines with no embell-
ishments, no skin, no personality. It reminds me of the
gowns worn in the 40s with buttons and fabric packed
up to her neck. In contrast, the first dresses were too
revealing. The sheer corsets revealing the secret tattoo
she'd gotten for James were a bit much for everybody.
Including James who had to be politely removed after
accusing the sales lady of "exposing all his goodies."
Ew.

"Mama, just try on Jaima's pick. All of these are garbagé,"
I sigh.
Initially I wanted to be jealous that Jaima found the perfect dress for *my* mama so easily, but I have to give it to
her. She's a taste maker through and through. Her style
and her home are perfectly curated. That makes me even
more curious about what lies in the gift bag. So when
Mama trots off the pedestal to try on the last dress, I peek
inside.

"What is this?" I whisper.
There's a sealed jar with a bow on it, surrounded by a field
of tissue paper. It's pretty, but I can't discern the contents
of it, and I don't want to risk accidentally spilling it all
over this cashmere carpet. It's too pristine. I'm sure it's

maintained by fairies or some shit.

"It's a cocktail mixer," Jaima explains. "I examined the notes of your whiskey and made a syrup based on the flavors. This one is a twist on amaretto sour. With raspberry puree and pear syrup."

I stare at the jar for what feels like hours. I was right in my initial concerns, because this gift is impossible to come close to.

Does she hate me or what?

"I don't know what to say," I admit with a gulp. "This is the most considerate thing I've received in recent years. Thank you. I wasn't expecting it."

"What?" Jaima asks with a wrinkled nose. "What were you expecting?"

"I don't know! Maybe a grocery store jar of pasta sauce. I didn't think you liked me!"

"Why would you think that?"

"Because you're always weirdly distant. We've seen each other twice and you look inconvenienced every time."

This conversation was ill timed because I could hear mama rustling around in the fitting room. Any second she would pop out looking like a regal queen, and I wanted all attention to be on her. But honestly I couldn't hold it in any longer than I had. We were facilitating a wedding together and I didn't thrive under passive aggressive awkwardness. So we needed to be big girls and figure this out.

"I don't dislike you!" Jaima argued. "I- I. Listen, Hen."

Jaima

What I want to say before Arnetta emerged was, *I'm attracted to you.* Instead all I do is stutter over the word I and stare at her with an open mouth before her mother's tearful expression recaptures our attention. Then I stay silent. Mostly because I can't tell her the truth now.

"Yes our parents are getting married and your mom looks very pretty in that dress, but I just thought you should know that I wanna suck your pussy like a pomegranate seed."

Daddy would clock me in the forehead with his oxford. That's an inside thought like a mother fucker.

So I stuff down my festering desires and focus on the podium. As awkward as the situation is, everything is worth it when I see Arnetta in that gown.

She's beyond stunning.

The fit is perfect by every inch, and the blush col-or compliments all the gentle warmth in her chocolate brown irises. She's graceful as she fans out the delicate, lace-trimmed skirt around her hips, and by the time her infectious smile reaches her eyes, I'm already texting Daddy to bring the Amex.

This is the dress.

"You look beautiful," Hen sniffles and I nod in agreement.

"How do you feel?" The associate asks.

"Gorgeous. Built like an IG baddie," Arnetta chuckles.

Just as she says that, Hen throws her hands into the air in defeat.

"I regret teaching you that phrase," she huffs.

"That's fine. I got other phrases. What's the thing y'all be saying? Bow. Bow. Bow."

My lips pucker against the force of a withheld laugh as Arnetta Brighton, a woman who could very well be a church mother, attempts to throw it back in her gown. I have to admit that for all the lace and fabric that she does it well. Even if Hen looks like she's about to slide out of her chair and melt into the floor from pure embarrassment.

Eventually the urge to cackle passes and when it does I immediately refocus on the logistics and practicality of the gown.

"Do you like how it fits?" I ask. "You're gonna be in it for quite a few hours."

"Mhm," Arnetta nods. "Although I am worried about having to use the ladies' room in it."

"Don't worry, they make something for that," I wave as I circle the podium.

I ordered the skirt lift the second she went back to try the dress on. Now I just have to make sure everything else is in order. The good thing is that nothing is digging into her skin or pinching at the seams and she looks like she has plenty of room to walk and sit. This is just a sample gown, but I doubt it'll need much alteration. It really is made for her.

"Is this the one?" Hen asks, focusing on the emotional. "Do you feel like the blushing bride you are?"

"I do," Arnetta cooes.

Hen comes to her mother's side and gently brushes away a slick tear before it can stain her collarbone. Suddenly I'm both grateful and jealous. I'll never be able to have a moment like this with my mom, but I'm happy to be included in this one.

"Sounds like we got a dress! I let Daddy know to heat up the card," I chuckle.

Suddenly Hen reaches into her front pocket and pulls out a wad of cash.

"Actually, I'll take care of it," she chuckles. "I had a great year, and you two are retired. Consider it a wedding gift. You deserve it, Mommy."

Arnetta wraps her arms around her daughter in a tearful sob and that's all it takes for a room full of women to burst into tears, me included. Mostly because I recognize Hen's love and generosity as a beautiful thing, and partly because I wish I could hug my own mother like that. However before the grief can pull me down too far, Arnetta snatches me into the huddle with a soft giggle.

"I really do love you girls," she whispers.

In the five years I've known Arnetta, she has never once made me feel other than. In fact I often felt at home around her. Even when she was just humming along to the radio and asking me about my week. Now though, with the infamous scent of White Diamonds and baby oil filling my nose as I finally let myself relax after a taxing month, I feel like I was always meant to be here.

I'm so glad Daddy didn't fuck this up.

"Ok, enough crying," I sigh. "This is not the good setting spray and I can't have my foundation running. We have 39 minutes of this appointment left and we need to try on at least two different styles of bridesmaid dresses."

Hen looks at me like I'm a puzzle she's trying to solve after my announcement, and although I feel slightly bad about it, the urge to bend her over the side table in my library grows. Why is her face so expressive? Lips shouldn't pout like that. It wasn't fair, and it made my nipples hard.

"Jaima is right," Arnetta affirms. "I found my dress but we

need to get you two in something. We don't have that much time to go."

With that, Hen goes off in search of something. I notice that she generally sticks to sale racks and clearance bins, and that's fine. However what's not fine is the cuts she's choosing. To keep shit a bean, Henrietta has a whole lot of ass. It's like a super moon, eye-catchingly enormous and sometimes hypnotizing. Full moons are beautiful, but trying to squeeze one in a champagne glass is crazy.

"Hey, Hen," I whisper as she pulls a dress from the rack. "Do you mind if I help you pick out a few things?"

"Actually I do. No offense, Jaima, but we haven't even interacted enough for you to know my style."

Ouch.

While she has a point, she hasn't counted on me occasionally stalking her social media. I know what she likes. Starting with gothic romance and ending with her black coffee with only a pump of whipped cream.

"And don't worry, it's not farmer chic," she says, motioning to her overalls.

Mama told me to try to live my life without regrets before she left, but I can't say I was honoring that very well at the moment. I had avoided Hen as much as possible within the last five years so I didn't develop a crush on my kinda step-sister, and now she hates me. Or at least finds me barely tolerable.

"Ok, just let me know if you change your mind," I sigh.

My gut does that thing to let me know that it's a bad idea to give up so easily, but it's either respect her decision or confess that I sometimes picture laughing with her over candlelit dinner in front of our parents.

Update:

It was a bad idea.

Because now we're three dresses and a whole lot of frustration in, and the fourth dress has ripped clean down Henrietta's ass. One quick movement to adjust her socks induced a parade of split seams and black lace thongs. It was awkward enough with the three of us, but of course that's when the store manager decided to check in on our appointment. Hen's near tears by the time she wiggles out of the mangled gown and dons regular clothes. It's not her fault, but I knew this would happen.

"Oh, baby. We can always try another store," Arnetta cooes.

"Exactly," I nod. "There's a formals boutique in the next plaza."

Hen looks at her mom's dress, already hanging on the purchase rack with the order number stapled to the garment bag. Her face twists with anguish while her shoulders drop in defeat. It's second nature for me to soothe her by rubbing her back, and for some reason she lets me.

"No, we're not gonna split up the orders like that," she sighs. "Everybody else found a dress and James' tux is here too. I will order something on my own but I'd rather them get started on everything else today. We only have nine months to go."

"Oh, did you already pick a date?" I ask our parents.

I'm still rubbing Hen's back at this point and she begins to sway along to the rhythm, her hips bumping mine. The gentle back and forth motion lulled me into a sort of mindless bliss. So I almost didn't hear my dad when he whispered,

"December 25th."

"Dec- Wait, Christmas!? You're getting married on Christmas?"

Anxiety rises in my chest, causing my heart to pound like a brass band drum. I never sweat but now I feel it sticking to my shirt, making the thin linen I'm wearing sheer with disappointment. Memories of tacky plaid dresses, crinoline bows, shedding tinsel, and flickering light displays assault me.

Fucking Christmas.

I hate it.

"Are you ok?" Hen asks while eyeing my drenched shirt.

"Jaima's, a bit of a... Christmas Grinch," Daddy explains with an apologetic grimace.

That's an understatement. I make the Grinch look like a pussy hoe. One year I stole a tree out of my dorm and sold it to our local art hippie. She made a ugly ass sculpture out of it; A dripping, spray-painted mess supposedly representing modern day capitalism. But I didn't care as long as I didn't have to look at it.

"Do we need to move the dates around?" Arnetta asks. "The venue might still be able to work with us."

"No!" I shout.

I could see the disappointment swell in her and Daddy's eyes as soon as she suggested it.

Yes I hate Christmas, but I love our parents. They've both accommodated enough for life's disappointments and If they wanna be holly, jolly, and in matrimony, I won't stop them. I'll suck it up and sing the shitty carols under the mistletoe with the rest of everyone else.

At least there will be eggnog.

"Don't change the date," I say quietly. "I'm just not a big fan of Christmas, but it's fine. This is your day and I want you to be happy. Candy canes and all."

Suddenly I'm catching myself from falling as Arnetta throws herself at me in a tight hug. She's crying again, and damnit all, she's got me sniffling too.

"Thank you, daughter," she cooes. "I promise this will be a good Christmas for all of us."

I hug her back because honestly it heals something in me to have regular human interaction, but I secretly remain unconvinced. Not because Arnetta doesn't mean it, but because I believe Christmas spirit is two cans of wallet Raid in a trench coat. For all my 31 years, I have learned that life has the tendency to be funny.

Especially around the holidays.

3

A DECENT PROPOSAL

Hen

I drape the last line of lights over the tree and flip the switch.

Glorious.

My house lights up like a LAX runway. The porch, the window trim, and my posts all glow a soft yellow while the house is a mix of loud reds, flickering greens, and pulsing purples. I know my electric bill will be through the roof, but I don't care. It's a small price to pay for a month of happiness. With the wedding literally right around the corner, Thanksgiving was hell. The food was good, don't get me wrong, however everyone was tense about our

upcoming schedule.
And Jaima...

I don't know what to think about Jaima. She's still quiet and distant a good 70% of the time, but every once and a while her walls will slip. When they do, her smiles grow softer and less rehearsed, her tone will become honeyed and undemanding, and the awkwardness between us melts into something else. A different type of tension. Something heart-pounding, skin-chilling, and slightly suffocating at times.

My best friend, Karlee, thinks I like her. Or rather that we like each other, but that doesn't make sense. We couldn't be more different. I'm chaotic and Jaima's too straight laced to have a crush on her almost step-sister.
Right?

The dress box lying in my closet might indicate otherwise. I received it from a white-glove courier four months ago. It came with a single stemmed rose and a hand-written card. One promising that the pristine gown tucked away inside would be a perfect fit for both my extra wide hips and my personality. I didn't believe it at first, but it was. Between the hints of ruched glitter mesh, the deep pockets, the dramatic hem, and artful pleats, it was everything I hoped for.

Which only causes more confusion. I now have a thousand questions surrounding Jaima Hines.

What the fuck is her deal? Does she regularly send expensive dresses to women she barely speaks to, or am I special? Why doesn't she like Christmas? Why does she know how to make a cocktail mixer, and will she make me more? Does she wanna kiss or should we just square up?

Suddenly my coffee machine dings, breaking me out of spiral. I was so deep in the equation that is me and Jaima's weird relationship that I completely forgot about my brew. I wait all year for a peppermint mocha with a dollop of whipped cream, and the only thing that stops me from drinking them earlier is the limited time stock. So I decide then and there that I'm going to stop obsessing over Jaima for five minutes and enjoy my beverage.

Yet as I sit into my worn recliner and kick my legs up, I find myself grabbing my phone and sending a message. We need to figure this out.

> Hey, would you like to get lunch today? I'm off at two.

Jaima

Lunch?

I stare at the message for the third time in the hour. I haven't technically opened it yet but I saw it as soon as she sent it. It's still at the top of my notification bar, marked as a priority.

"Jaima," Dolly cooes before sipping her tea. "It's just lunch."

Her elegant hand slips underneath mine forcing me to click on the message and mark it as read. Everybody thinks Maia is the one to watch in our group, but it's quiet, church mouse Cindy. Nicknamed Dolly, her features are soft and pouty. A perfect juxtaposition to her sometimes sharp personality. She's too keen for her own good, or ours for that matter.

"I can't hookup with my dad's wife's daughter!" I protest.
As if that was even a suggestion, but still.

"What a round about way of saying step-sister," Cindy
chortles. "However, nobody said anything about confess-
ing your feelings and riding off into the sunset. It's just
lunch, babe."

Yeah it was just lunch until Hen started dancing when
she took the first bite of her food, I inevitably stared,
she called me out, and then we kissed over a shared
hummus plate. Then I'd be in a wedding party with her
three weeks later, probably heart broken, and without
enough powder to keep tears from streaking my makeup.

"You know what your problem is? You think too much."
She gives me a pointed look as she spreads the throw I've
been eyeing for the last thirty minutes over our legs. I
would've gotten it earlier, but I didn't want to mess up
her display. Does that prove her point? Yes, but that's not
my fault.

"I get paid to think, Doll."

"Yes, you get paid to think Monday through Friday, seven
to three. It's ten AM on a Saturday morning, and your big
booty step-sister, whose Instagram you regularly stalk,
just asked you to lunch. What exactly is there to think
about?"

"Well our parents for one," I protest.

"Booo! Y'all are all grown."

"She's kinda famous."

"We live in LA, baby. Everyone here is kinda famous."

"Ok, but Hen has tattooed half of today's recording artists, and probably even the Pope."

"So what! You program super computers."

"That's not as cool in conversation!"

"Who cares!? You're fine as fuck, and young, and obviously you too like each other."

"Henrietta doesn't like me."

"Fine, if that's the case, lunch should be easy. I told her you'll meet her at her shop at 1:30. You better go touch up your makeup and pick out something cute."

Suddenly my time management software comes online. I need to leave now if I'm going to change, reapply my makeup, and get to West Hollywood by 1:30. Church traffic will be horrible by twelve.

"I cannot stand you!" I hiss as I shuffle to collect my purse and leave.

"Love you too. Send me an update after!" Dolly giggles.

"No!" I fuss, even though we both know I definitely will. Because Hen already made reservations for my favorite restaurant.

Hen

"You're too big to be doing all of this," I chide as I finish shading. "This is your twelfth tattoo."

Donovan Dame is a lineman for the LA Sharks. He's six foot seven, 289 pounds of pure muscle, and although he doesn't look like it, he's also a gigantic baby. All this sniffling is unnecessary. We did a small name for his newest niece. It took less than an hour from start to finish and I wasn't even touching him with the needle half of the time.

"Damn, Henny. We all ain't gangsta like you. You draw on yourself when you get bored."

Yeah I did, but even still.

"Big man, you get paid to knock the wind out of mother fuckers. This is barely a scratch."

He rolls his eyes as he checks out his "scratch" in the mirror, but he doesn't argue. So once he gives me his approving nod, I clean the excess ink off his arm, refrain from laughing at his dramatic flinch, then apply a second skin.

"All done!"

"Good cause I go-"

"Oh I'm sorry. Am I interrupting?" Jaima interjects.

She's still standing in the door of my shop when I look up, legs out, hair pulled high, sun casting a halo around her lithe frame as she twiddles her fingers.

And all I can do is stare.

Until Donovan opens his mouth.

"Hell nah, you ain't interrupting shit!" he shouts. "What's your name, baby?"

"Unavailable," I grit out harsher than intended.

I have to remind myself to relax when I find myself reaching for my blade. I feel like a cat hissing over fresh meat but I really can't pinpoint why. It's not just because Jaima's face scrunched up right the second he asked, although that does play a big part. I lit on fire the second he set his eyes on her. Maybe I'm jealous?

"Damn my bad, Hen. I ain't know you had a girl. No harm, no foul."

I want to protest before this gets out of hand, but Donovan has already slipped me double what he owes and left by the time I realize the implications of my outburst. So now I'm just standing in the middle of my shop, looking like a sister-fucker. A Step-sister fucker. God, is my life a porn category?

"You look pretty today," Jaima whispers as I try to regain my bearings.

"Thank you," I whisper while looking at my crop top and cargos. "So do you."

Jaima looks like someone studied a hibiscus at peak bloom for months on end and then rendered it into a human being. She has her usual highlight and soft pastel lip color, but today is one of the rare occasions I see her outside of a pantsuit. The dress she's wearing is a long sleeved bodycon situation with burgundy and pink ombre. It pairs perfectly with the white strappy heels she has on, and of course her perfectly painted bright red toes.

Not gonna lie, I'd try it too if I were Donovan.

"Hen?" Jaima yells, jostling me from my impure thoughts.

"Hm?"

"Are you ready? I can drive if you want."

"Yeah sure. Let me just grab my purse and we can go."

I agreed enthusiastically, but as I locked up the shop and followed the Amazonian goddess to her souped up drop-top, I couldn't help but think this was a bad idea.

"That was a terrible idea," Jaima whispers over the top of her menu.

I gradually shift my gaze to the couple she's talking about. I guess it was an attempt at a public break-up, but the woman is drop dead gorgeous while the guy looks like a boiled hotdog. So after he broke the news, she knocked back her merlot and went to flirt at the bar. So far she has snagged two handsome older men with big watches and custom suits. Love that for her.

"I did not expect you to be a people watcher," I chuckle.

If it wasn't for Jaima, I would've completely missed the show. Same thing with the drive over. It also had lots of commentary.

"I can't help it," she giggles. "It's in my genes. James is very nosey."

"Is he really?"

"Yes! That man sat up and did a whole investigation into my ex because she said she was taking a break from dating for her mental health and then popped out married. He had a whole connection web in my library. It turns out her wife was in the closet for years before they got married. It was insane."

At this point my laughter is shaking the table. I don't know which part of the story is crazier, but I gotta give James his props. I think he might be a better detective than most women alive.

"Ok but technically she didn't lie. She did take a break from dating."

"You hush," Jaima chides with muted laughter. "That was almost my villain origin story."

"Almost? Baby I would've crashed the honeymoon. Y'all hungry? Let's go see what the buffet is serving."

"I thought about it. But they traveled during hurricane season and got stranded in Curacao so I felt vindicated."

"As you should," I cackle.

We descend into a loaded silence, but again it's not the awkward one I've come to expect. Instead it's full of desire, hope, and curiosity made evident with raised brows and half hung lips. Jaima's lips are open into a soft o while mine are pinched between my teeth.

Shit.

I think I might like my step-sister.

"Can I interest you ladies in any dessert?" The waiter asks. "We just started serving our Christmas classics."

I'm more than positive that something on the menu contains gingerbread so I'm ready to say absolutely, but I don't miss the tiny frown and accompanying scoff that comes from Jaima.

"Can we please look at a dessert menu?" I say.

"Sure, take your time. I'll be back in a bit to check on you."

He sits down the fancy gold leaf menu and departs, leaving me to why we're really here.

"Why do you hate Christmas?" I ask bluntly.

"I- I don't *hate* it," Jaima replies weakly. "It's just not my favorite time of year. It's high stress, high cost, and honestly too loud. The end of the year should be relaxing."

"Christmas can be plenty relaxing."

"Getting your toes run over by some juiced-up, super couponer's over-packed cart in Arrowfield's is not relaxing."

"Ok first off, why are you not getting things delivered? Once it's past two PM, the stores are dead to me this time of year."

"They never get the produce right," she shrugs. "And if it's a man? Ain't no lemons, you're getting a lightbulb."

Of course we erupt into another fit of giggles. It takes me almost falling out of the chair to regain my composure and when I do, Jaima's watching me with that same hopeful, affectionate gaze. A gaze I could see myself swimming in under different circumstances.

Maybe after all of this is done.

"Let me prove you wrong," I whisper.

"About GroceryGo? Henny, please."

"No, I don't take losing bets. Let me prove you wrong about Christmas."

"Hen, I say this with respect, that's impossible."

"You don't know that for sure," I protest. "I have a plan."

"A plan?"

"Yes, first we order the mulled cherry cheesecake with the gingerbread crust. Then next week we do Christmas break for grown ups. I know you got PTO to burn."

"I gotta take off?" Jaima pouts.

"You need to take off anyway. You go on like one vacation a year."

She looks like she might protest but I give her a firm, yet playful look letting her know that I know better. She blocks her vacation off eight months in advance on James and Mama's family calendar. We also got email reminders.

"Fine, what will we be doing?" she relents.

"It's a surprise. I'll text you suggested attire the night before though, and you'll get a location the morning of if I don't pick you up."

Jaima Hines is a planner, all the way down to her pressed socks and meticulously styled suits. So when she brings her manicured nails to the sides of her temples, I just know she's gonna say no. However, looks can be deceiving.

"Why do I feel like I'm gonna regret this?"

"Ignore that feeling, it's wrong!" I laugh triumphantly. "We're gonna have a great time. Starting now with that cheesecake. Oh, waiter!"

4
Suit Up

Jaima

Damn that was some good cheesecake. All tart, buttery, and creamy. A week has passed since I ate it, and I still think about it every hour on the hour. Hen told me to get a to-go order, but I didn't want that temptation in the house. It's bad enough I'm spending the week with her unchaperoned. Especially after I stared at her with hearts in my eyes over lunch.

Part of me wants to cancel, but a bigger part is begging to spend more time with Hen. She's unexpected. Still vibrant and outgoing, but with an air of tenderness I can't quite place. At this point, I fully accept that I have a crush on her. There's nothing that can be done about that. However, fanning the flames of desire with a week of quality time is certainly a choice.

Probably a bad one.

My phone vibrates with a text. Hen is outside in my driveway and although I've dressed myself a million times before, I suddenly question if I'm doing it wrong. My makeup is perfect today, my slacks are pressed, and my shoes
are on the right feet but I feel like I'm missing something.
Unfortunately I can't give it too much thought because
we have a two hour drive ahead of us.

I climb into the passenger side of Hen's Rav4 with a
tepid smile, and she immediately holds out a brown sugar
matcha from my favorite spot up the street.

"Oh, thank you. Good morning by the way."

"Good morning," she nods as she gives me a once over. "I
have a quick question. Are you wearing a suit?"

"You said to dress warm! It's wool."

"I said to dress warm and comfy," she chides.

"Suits are comfy. This one has a soft inner lining and
relaxed seams."

"Eventually I have to introduce you to 4-way stretch material, but it's fine. I can work with this for now. Buckle up,
buttercup! We got two hours to get in the holiday mood."

I don't know what I expect, but it isn't a curated Black
Christmas playlist. Still I won't complain. The ride up to
Big Bear is full of spirited crooning of Luther Vandross,
Mariah Carey, and Stevie Wonder. I'm almost disappoint-
ed when we arrive and the engine cuts while I'm on the
bridge of 8 Days Of Christmas.

But then I notice Hen staring at me.

"I could watch you sing all day," she says wistfully, after

being noticed. "Just not today. Look alive, Jaima! We're going ice skating!"

Again, the planner in me wants to protest. I'm woefully under prepared for something like this. However before I could say my piece, Hen pops the trunk to reveal a brand new pair of size 10.5 ice skates, and padding extraordinaire.

"I know you don't like renting shoes because you worry about contracting fungal infections, so I got these for you. James told me you're a big Sanrio fan."

In disbelief, I run my fingers over the embroidered design of Cinnamon Roll. Every detail is perfect, down to the pop of baby pink in the laces.

Usually I try to keep my demeanor cool, but not today. Today I let the gratitude overtake me before I turn around to give Hen a big squeeze.

"Oh, you give good hugs," she whispers while squeezing me back.

She doesn't know that it's making it harder for me to let her go, and I don't tell her either. I just enjoy the moment for however long it lasts and thank God that I didn't cancel.

This will be fun.

Update:

It's not fun. My legs are too long, and I'm too overconfident for this shit. I knew ice wouldn't be easy, but I didn't expect to wobble like a giraffe calf the entire time either. Hen is holding onto my arm, pulling me along with ease. Meanwhile I'm literally shaking in my boots.

"You gotta relax, Jaima," she cooes. "I'm not gonna let you fall."

I know Hen means well, but I can't find it in my rickety joints to believe her with all the people flying past us.

"Relax," she says again. "You're too stiff and it's going to make turning difficult. Just focus on something pretty and drop your weight into your legs."

That advice is helpful. I slowly release my tense muscles and lean on my thighs for support. All while focusing on Henrietta. She's blissfully unaware of me though. Instead she's looking at all the twinkling lights draped around the rink, the snow capped pines, and the tips of the nearby mountain ranges. As she smiles, it begins to flurry. Tiny, delicate snowflakes cascade down from the overcast sky and land in the tips of her lashes and the roots of her locs, making her look angelic. Suddenly my steps falter and we tumble together before catching each other's arms for balance.

"I know it doesn't look like it right now, but you were doing really good," Hen giggles.

I adjust my grip on her arms, and that one little movement threatens to send us crashing into the polished ice.

"I think you're a liar," I sigh. "We're about to eat the curb."

"Ha, we're fine. Just lean onto me and I'll straighten us out."

Inch by inch, I adjust until Hen's front is flush with mine. If I wasn't freezing my ass off I might find our positioning awkward, but right now I'm focused on not falling. Eventually we're upright though. Hen's hands are on my waist and back and my hands mirror hers. Merry Little Christmas starts pouring out of the speakers positioned around the rink, encouraging us to rock along, and for a moment everything feels perfect. Despite all my reluctance, this feels like exactly where I'm meant to be. Spinning on ice in the middle of the California mountains with Henrietta tucked against my chest, as snow floats down from the heavens above. I don't even care that my undies are likely frozen.

"Are you two girlfriends?" A small child asks.

He's got to be no more than five judging by his chubby cheeks and slightly sticky hands. He looks at me and Hen with all the innocent childlike wonder in the world as he awaits our answer, occasionally motioning to the way we're hugging. My heart tugs because I always wanted to be a mom, and for a split second I imagine what me and Hen's baby would look like. Probably the same rich shade of brown as the little boy in front of us, but with Hen's gap and maybe my freckles.

"No, we're not girlfriends," Hen giggles. "We're just friends."

Exactly. Just friends. Friends. Friends. Fucking friends.

"Oh ok. My dads are boyfriends!" he explains before two worried men rush behind him.

"Jonathan, your dads are husbands," one sighs. "Sorry ladies, we passed our love of yapping down to our youngest."

"We don't mind," Hen and I answer simultaneously.

Then we hit each other with,

"Jinx!"

Jonathan's parents look at us like we're floating down a river called Denial about just being friends, while Jonathan happily spins around them. I can feel the queer judgement seeping underneath my coat, but Hen holds me steady, returning their stare double-time.

"Well you two have a great day," the other dad says. "We're sorry for interrupting."

"It's no problem at all! Bye, Jonathan!" I call.

"Bye giant lady. Bye tinier lady!" he belts back.

Me and Hen blink a few times in disbelief before she starts to slowly pull us back to the railing. Somehow we spent almost two hours on the ice, and now we're starving. First though, we have to get these skates off.

"Who do you think he was calling a giant lady?" she asks. "Obviously me."

"Pftt. You're not giant. You're just tall. I'm like two of you across."

"Is that what makes you a giant?"

"Duh."

"Henny, I say this with all the love in the world. The only thing giant on you is your ass and thighs."

"You think this ass fat?" she teases while throwing it in a small circle.

I know it was meant to be a joke but my mind and jaw went slack. She was popping that shit for all of three seconds, but somehow it turned into a feature-length film in my memories. It was terrible timing really. Every other function my brain normally performed was out of the window, and eventually I had to sit down on the trail to keep from blacking out. Even then, my breath was still coming out in quick spurts while bright-white spots occlude my vision.

"Shit, Jaima! I did not mean to keep you out this long," Hen hisses. "Come on, let's go eat."

Hen

"Are you sure you don't need to see the nurse? We have a day pass for a reason."

"Hen, I'm fine. My blood sugar was just low."

"Ok," I agree hesitantly. "Let me know if anything changes."

"Worry wart," Jaima teases while sipping her rescue cocoa.

She could tease all she wanted to, but when she dropped to the ground my heart dropped right along with her. That was the first time I've ever seen her completely disengage from reality and it was terrifying. Her eyes were glossy and glazed over. Her mouth was open yet no words were coming out. She just puffed out a soft, disjointed sigh as she tried to catch her breath. Luckily I asked James if she had any health issues the week before so I knew about her hypoglycemia.

"I will be adjusting the rest of our scheduled activities for snack breaks, since you obviously won't tell me when you need to eat," I grumble.

"I'm sorry! I thought I had time. I had oatmeal and sausage before we left."

"Jaima, that was five hours ago!"

"Really? We've been out that long?"

I don't want to rain on her parade or toot my own horn by telling her I was right about my Christmas break idea. But I was definitely right. She was so relaxed that she hadn't even noticed the afternoon creeping up despite all the kids and chaos surrounding us. Including the two dads who were eyeing us expectedly from across the lodge's lobby.

"They think we're lipstick lesbians," I whisper.

"Technically they're right about me," Jaima murmurs, keeping her mouth down in her cocoa mug.

I don't dare acknowledge that new lore. Because the second I do, it's guaranteed to blow up our whole week if not our entire month. The last thing I need is to be coordinating a wedding with a woman I want to fuck. Especially a woman who's directly related to the man my mom is marrying.

"Are you ready to order lunch?" I ask. "I can get us menus."

"I already ordered our entrees and appetizers on the app," Jaima shrugs. "I got you the dairy-free pesto cavatappi with smoked chicken breast and an order of calamari for the table. Extra lemon."

"Who told you I was lactose intolerant?" I ask, narrowing my eyes.

"You mentioned it about three years ago in passing. I try to be mindful."

Three years ago? I can barely remember the conversations I had yesterday. I'm impressed, but I also stressed, because I never wanted to kiss another person so bad in my life. All the thoughtfulness and consideration women expected from men was tripled in other women. On one hand it made the heartbreak worse if and when it happened, but on the other it was like a honey salve for your soul when you found the right person. For some reason, my mouth tastes sweet as I watch Jaima's sly smirk.

"I'm going to let this slide because those two men from the rink keep watching us like we're about to kiss, but we will be having a conversation about you and what you know later," I say.

"Will we?" Jaima teases with her eyes dropping low.

"Yes, we will. We need to talk through whatever this is."

"That's not what I was referring to, but sure. We can talk about it. Just not right now cause the food's coming." There was a giant, hot plate of calamari in my face before I could process what Jaima meant, and even after I do I'm too hungry to revisit the conversation. However, now I know for sure. My kinda step-sister has a crush on me. And I like her back.

Of course Jaima falls asleep as soon as we hit the highway.

Talk about it my ass.

Still it's fine. I had a great day with her despite the light flirting that made my heart skip around. Jaima is so much more than the dedicated engineer she presents to the general public. From her keen observation skills, to her high notes, and wine pairings, she's remarkable. Even when she's knocked out in the passenger seat and snoring like a cartoon mouse after a day in the mountains.

"Hey," I say while gently rubbing her arm. "We're here."

We had been parked in her driveway for ten minutes, but I couldn't bring myself to wake her for the first five, and the second half had been spent with me watching drool pool in the corner of her mouth.

"Damn, I fell asleep?" she groans. "Sorry, Hen. I know I snore."

"It's fine," I shrug, withholding the fact that I thought it was cute. "We had a long day."

"Yeah, but I had a really nice time with you. Thanks for planning this."

She flashes me a soft, innocent smirk that once again leaves me flustered. I don't know what it is about this woman. I've had girlfriends in the past. I've dealt with my fair share of toxic instalove. But something about being around Jaima when the world isn't watching leaves me shaking.

"Oh, um. It's no problem. Just wait until tomorrow."

"Yeah I can't wait until tomorrow. Goodnight, Henny."

"Goodnight, Jaima," I mumble, hoping to sound calm.

I know I don't pull it off though because she giggles after

pressing a quick kiss to my cheek.

I'm fucked.

5
D&D

Jaima

I don't date much.

Besides the fact that I'm socially awkward, I'm also easily taken advantage of. It's something that my mom pointed out about me a long time ago. I will give until I'm bleeding. I got a good group of friends who keep me levelheaded though. I'm never desperate for sex, or attention, or companionship. So I can afford the emotional and tedious task of vetting a potential partner. It usually takes me months to decide I want to date someone. Several outings and conversations to gauge how well we would mesh. I needed to be able to picture quiet moments and lazy evenings with them. However after spending one day with Hen, I could tell that loving her would eventually be as easy as breathing.

I can't quite explain what did it. Maybe it was the matcha, or the custom skates, or maybe it was the way she responded when I had an episode. Calm but still urgent. Attentive. Kind. Prepared because she reached out to Daddy beforehand.

It was all very different from most women I dated. Mostly because they were all terrible in emergency situations. There's a reason James Hines was still my emergency contact. However I'm ready for that era to come to an end.

I'm ready to get a girlfriend.

"Hey, what are we doing today?" I ask.

Hen passes me another bev before she answers. Today it's apple cider with a salted caramel and vanilla cold foam. It tastes suspiciously like a holiday and it's very addictive. Which is crazy because I usually hate holiday drinks.

"I knew you would like it," she whispers before handing me a sheet of paper out the console. "Anyway, we're doing a workshop. Circle three activities you wanna do."

I'm not exactly sure how to narrow it down to just three. The list is extensive, with everything from Santa archery to a scarf knitting class. Yet my hand moves automatically when I see candle making listed as an option. That lady loved her candles. It feels like a sign.

"These three," I whisper as if it's a secret.

Hen carefully slides the paper from my grip and although she doesn't say much, her eyes smile.

"Okie dokie. Seatbelt please."

"Roger," I say while reaching for both my belt and the volume dial. "I'm excited."

"You should be. Because after our workshop, I'm introducing you to stretch knit."

I roll my eyes. I knew I should've worn something different yesterday, but honestly I didn't have a lot of warm clothes because the only time I traveled to cold places was for work.

"You wear one suit out to an activity and suddenly it's you don't know comfort."

"You're wearing a blazer right now, sweetness," she teases.

"Hey, I'm layering. The blazer provides a little structure to the jumpsuit since it's so flowy. Let me cook."

"I'll never shit on a baddie," Hen protests while merging onto the 105. "However, what I will say is that every baddie needs a pair of stretchy pants. Pants that are giving couch potato."

"I've never seen you in couch potato pants."

"Yes, that's because I have the illusion of being put together. I have on actual clothes for maybe eight hours a day max, and then the rest of the time I'm a bare faced Black Winnie The Pooh."

I immediately imagine Hen lounging on the couch, her feet tucked under her shapely thighs with her nipples visible through the thin cotton of a cropped tee. All that rich brown skin on display. All those supple curves...

"Sorry, I need a Xanax," I explain as I shuffle through my purse.

My heart is pounding in my ears as I search for my pill case. I can't believe I'm taking rescue meds before ten, but that vision sent me over the edge. If Hen accidentally brushes against me before I pop one, I'm at risk of blacking out. Everybody thinks that anxiety is some monster exclusive to dark times, but it's with me always. Even when I'm just excited about a pretty woman.

"Do you need us to pull over?" she asks calmly.

"No, no. It's not the drive. I'm just-"

Honestly, I'm at risk of ruining my underwear. I can't tell her that though. That's a terrible segue into courtship. "I *wanna date you so bad that I'm having a panic attack*," is one of those things that's cute in books but worrisome in real life.

"I'm having a little moment," I try to explain.

Hen taps something on her display and classical music begins pouring through the car seconds later.

Now my body is confused about what to do. The soft piano riffs are relaxing, but my brain is freaking out because I'm probably sitting next to my future wife. Hen doesn't know she's my future wife though, so she thinks she's being casual when she slides her hand up and down my arm. Meanwhile I'm literally about to combust.

"Hey, please don't take this the wrong way, but I need you to stop touching me," I whisper.

Her hand snaps back to her side of the car immediately. She doesn't say anything besides a soft sorry, but I can tell my tone hurt her.

Shit.

I need to get it together.

Hen

The North Pole Village is a pop-up located in Melrose. It's hosted by a slew of local artists and instructors, and the money goes to support local charities. Which means they usually have sponsors and go all out. Including the elf prosthetics on the hostesses and guides.

"Welcome to Santa's Workshop!" the hostess cheers.

Jaima immediately bristles beside me. Unlike yesterday. Yesterday went so well. I thought we were making progress, but then she had a panic attack when we rode past the giant wreath on Alameda. I guess it was just one ornament too many? I don't really know. I wish she would tell me what's going on so I can help her through it. Instead she's shutting down behind her curtain of mystery.

"What do you wanna do first?" I ask, hoping to break Jaima from her nervous observations.

"Axe throwing," she answers without hesitation.

I get no time to process that before I'm being pulled along, to the map in the center of the makeshift village. Jaima quickly locates the hosting area, and then whisks us away. Her expression remains closed off and resolute.

"Did all the decorations overwhelm you?" I ask as we don gloves and protective gear.

Although she seems less tense, I'm still trying to understand what happened. We were laughing one minute and anxious the next.

"Hm? Oh, Hen no. It's just- I'm really bad at this," Jaima sighs.

"Listen, I know we have to ease you into everything. But just-"

"Ease me into what?"

"The Christmas spirit."

Jaima's eyes quickly dart to the floor and then back to

mine twice before she puffs out a relieved breath and refocuses on our activity.

"Right, ok. We're easing me into the Christmas spirit. Now let's decapitate some Santas."

Jaima is an enigma.

Quiet, shy, graceful, and secretly violent like an Ogun warrior. She didn't miss not one target. She actually took out all of hers and two of mine. Then she screamed in victory when she crushed the bonus round. I don't know how the staff is feeling after watching that display, but I'm traumatized.

"Hey," I start as I sit down with our snacks. "Is work going ok?"

She tears into the ham toasty voraciously,

"Yeah, why do you ask?"

"No, reason in particular. It's just, that was terrifying and I think it could be potentially used against you in a court of law."

"The axing?"

"Yeah, the axing."

"I probably should've warned you that at one point I was slated to join the Air Force," she chuckles.

That explains a lot honestly. Especially Jaima's unwavering punctuality. I wonder what made her choose computer engineering instead?

"Changed your mind?"

"Uh, kinda. My mom got sick around the time I was supposed to be leaving for bootcamp. I couldn't delay my departure, so I ended up saying fuck it and going Kingford instead."

So that's what made her choose engineering instead.

"You're a good daughter," I say softly. "I know your mom was and remains so proud."

"Thank you. I hope so," Jaima sniffles.

I abandon my churro, wipe my sugar-dusted fingers, and then blot Jaima's tears away.

"No crying today, pretty girl. We can do that on our movie marathon day."

"God, Hen. What are you gonna have us watching?" she groans.

"That's for me to know and you to find out. Now who's ready to go make a candle?"

Jaima

"We have two wax types. Would you like our coconut-soy blend or the body safe shea blend?"

"I'll take the body safe one," Hen replies with a big grin.

The instructor then looks at me expectedly. Like she knows what type of time everyone is on, but the only thing I know about candles is that you can burn them.

"Uh, I'll take the coconut blend," I say.

I wait for her to walk off for our portioned wax chips before I ask Hen,

"What the fuck is the body safe one?"

"Oh it's low temp wax so it doesn't burn skin when dripped."

"Damn, should I have picked that? That sounds safe."

"It's a sex thing, Jaima," Hen giggles.

"Oh."

Part of me wants to text Cindy or maybe Velma to figure out how pouring hot wax on somebody is a sex thing. But the other part of me, the part that's already planned me and Hen's first official date, is absolutely devastated that she has plans for her candle.

"You and your girlfriend must have fun," I cackle nervously.

Hen gives me a pointed look that I don't care to acknowledge before she erupts into table shaking laughter.

"Now, Jaima," she chides. "You know good and well I don't have a girlfriend. What woman do you know who's going to let her girl skate chest to chest with someone else all day?"

"You never know," I shrug. "LA has a lot of polycules."

"Is this you inviting me into your polycule? If so, I'm not very good at D&D. I'm gonna tell you that right now."

"Damn! I know I'm a nerd, but D&D? Really, Hen?"

"Hey! You never know. That seems like a contingency of most harems today."

Before I can get my grievances off my chest, the class instructor returns with our wax and selected scents. She's wearing that same smile, although this time it's less coy and more, *meet me after class.*

"Here you are, ladies," she sings. "I hope you enjoy melting with me."

Her hips not so subtly bump our table when she walks away. Hen's pretending not to notice her obvious flirtation, but I can't pass up this opportunity.

"Is she in your polycule?" I ask with a smirk.

"Jaima, cut it out," she laughs back.

"I'm just asking. I wanna see what I'm up against. Who I'm *melting* for."

We both erupt into laughter. It lasts for what feels like five minutes and we only stop because we notice all the eyes on us instead of the instructor. Seriously, it's like being in a room full of owls.

"You will pay for your crimes," Hen whispers before returning to her wax. "Now focus."

The actual mixing part is straight forward and very relaxing. I can fall asleep stirring candle wax if not for the Rock N' Roll Christmas music pumping through the room. Once we've achieved the right consistency, we mix our scents in a little paper cup. Hen offers me a sniff of her concoction, and while I was skeptical at first, everything works well together.

"This smells like a peppermint mocha," I say.

"Mhm, it's my favorite drink. Mind if I smell yours?"

I scooch the cup towards her and her shoulders relax as she takes a big sniff.

"This smells so familiar," she whispers. "What is it?"

"I based it off my Mama's favorite perfume," I explain. "They don't make it anymore, but I was able to pull the fragrance notes off of one of her empty bottles so I wanted to see if I could recreate it."

"Have you ever worn it before?" Hen asks gently.

"Yeah, you probably smelled it on me when we went to look at dresses. I just missed her that day. Don't get me wrong, I love Arnetta-"

"Hey, I get it. Don't feel like you have to explain that kind of grief to me unless you want to. It's normal for you to want her there with you during big moments. I want my dad with me all the time."

My arms are wrapping around the woman in front of me for the third time this week. Between her and Arnetta,

I haven't hugged this much in years. It's kind of weird to think about. However with Hen the realization is less jarring. Hugging her feels like salve, gooey and healing.

"Thank you for this," I whisper.

"It's no problem," Hen says as she returns my squeeze.

Eventually we untangle and return to our candles. Keeping the wicks even during pouring is harder than I thought, but I'm proud of my little lopsided baby. I'm kind of bummed that we can't take them home immediately, but Hen has already filled out the shipping slips so we'll get them by the weekend.

"What time is the next hot chocolate lab?" I ask as we wander around the square.

Here, vendors are selling everything from bath products, to jewelry, winter snacks, and adult toys. Normally I wouldn't bat an eye at the variety, but then I see a guy twirling one in the corner stall.

"Is he selling cactus shaped dildos?"

"Yes," Hen nods. "They're surprisingly good quality."

I want to ask her how she knows that, but she changes the subject after studying my expression.

"Anyway we got an hour until the hot chocolate lab. So do you wanna get burgers?"

"Burgers sound good," I nod.

The savory scent of griddled meat and greasy fries lures me forward, but we're stopped by a series of urgent texts before we can reach nirvana. I hope it's just a sale text or something, but instead I open our family group chat to see our parents in hysterics.

"What does she mean it's gone?" I ask with a grimace.

"I don't know, but James asked us to meet them," Hen

mumbles while looking between the burger stand and her phone.

"Come on, we'll grab something the way there," she finally says, making a difficult decision for both of us.

Our lungs simultaneously puff with a hungry sigh as we head to the car.

And here I was thinking today would be a good day.

Hen

What do you do when a caterer you paid a deposit to a year in advance shuts down three weeks before your wedding?

Step one: Wail.

Step two: Cuss.

We're well past step two, so Jaima and I are in full fix it mode. With her on the phone with her lawyer friend, and me thumbing through my contacts to see if I could find somebody to handle a 300 person catering gig ASAP. I do find someone, but now we have to contact the venue and ask them to approve the new caterer. Since they suggested one left us an empty storefront and an IOU.

It takes us about an hour to sort everything out, but we get Karlee's uncle Kenny to handle catering, and Jaima's friend Cindy to handle the lawsuit.

I miss when my biggest issue of the day was the overly flirtatious candle maker shooting her shot at Jaima.

"Thank you, girls," Mama cooes. "We're so lucky to have two resourceful daughters."

That statement makes me cringe. Mostly because it reminds me how me and Jaima met. Through our engaged, soon-to-be married parents.

"It's no problem at all," Jaima says easily.

She gives Mama one of those tender and genuine smiles that makes my belly flip and I get the overwhelming urge to peck her in her pretty mouth.

"Where are y'all coming from?" James asks while looking at our wristbands.

"Santa's Workshop," I reply.

I don't know why I expect our parents to be updated on current events, but I should know they're not. Especially when both Mama and James frown up like I said we just popped over from visiting our favorite gloryhole.

"I really hate to ask, but before I request details, is that a sex thing?" he whispers nervously.

"Daddy!" Jaima chides as Mama pops him on the shoulder. "Why would you ask that?"

"I wanted to be sure! LA is a wild place!" he protests.

We spend about an hour with our parents before the hangry demon overtakes us and starts demanding things like overpriced chips and questionable street fruit. I almost buy a pineapple cup from the guy who is known for old strawberries, but Jaima politely excuses us before it gets to that point.

"God, I was starving," I groan while unwrapping my double.

"Me too. We would've disintegrated dealing with that man. I love my dad but he's a yapper. He talks so much he doesn't even remember what he was originally talking about."

I try not to laugh while I savor the first bite. It's crispy from the fresh jalapenos and onions with the cheese highlighting and harmonizing with the salted meat.

"Mama doesn't care," I chuckle. "You remember his Nebraska trip last year? She called me upset on the second day because she realized she couldn't sleep without hearing his late night rants. She ended up calling him and they chatted about a comet he was tracking. Speaking of comets, guess what I found out?"

"What, lovely?"

"Comets usually have two tails. They point in opposite directions. One is made of plasma. You know what else is made of plasma?"

"Blood?"

"Oh, yes. But fire too. There are actually four states of matter and plasma is one of them. Wait, what was I talking about again?"

"Comets, Hen."

"Right."

I look up from my half-eaten burger to spot Jaima, head in her hands as she watches me. Eyes full of genuine interest and amusement. Just like how Mama looks at James.

"Shit, our parents are about to get married," I whisper, realizing how similar we are to them.

The reminder shakes Jaima for her peaceful gazing and she sits up straight. Flustered and slightly annoyed.

"I know, in three weeks."

"Isn't that weird?" I say.

I don't know why I say it. A big part of me is just hoping she'll say fuck it and admit that she feels the same way about me that I feel about her. I hope she'll tell me I'm not crazy for constantly thinking about how we skated chest to chest with the snow falling all around us. I need her to tell me that the sparks I feel every time we brush hands aren't just in my head. I don't want it to matter, but I feel like it might.

"It is weird," she sighs while nibbling on a tot.

"But I'm happy for them."

"Me too."

"So what are we doing tomorrow?" Jaima asks, quickly changing the subject.

"Well tomorrow is a rest day. I know you need your recharge days."

"I really appreciate that," Jaima mumbles with a lovelorn smile.

"But Thursday, we party!"

"Shit."

I can see the fear in her eyes, however, I hope to turn it into wonder and joy. I got a little distracted by the deep cupid's bow of her top lip, but my mission still stands. We're going to un-Grinch Jaima Hines.

"Don't worry. It'll be fun. I got everything planned."

"Yay."

6
MERRY CHRISTMAS, BITCH

J aima

If I could've found a Grinch suit for the occasion, I would've worn it. Unfortunately the best I could do is a Scrooge tophat and accompanying nametag. The rest of the week was wonderful, but the brunt of my issues with Christmas lies in the parties. They're too loud, too messy, and too much. They're everything I work to avoid, and yet here I am, outside of the venue with blue highlight on my cheekbones and a ticket in hand. Honestly, if not for the massive heart-breaking crush I have on Hen, I wouldn't be here. Instead, I'd be in bed, rubbing my feet together, and eating fancy cheese.

God, that woman even has me talking in rhymes.

I've danced around how I'm feeling for long enough. I'm thinking about Hen in the morning when I take my first sip of coffee, in the afternoon when I turn on her playlists, and in the evening when I close my eyes and imagine her tucked against my chest, her fingers intertwined with my own. I even start to wonder how she would unwrap her first Christmas gift. Would she be slow and careful, or excited and quick? Would she hug me after, or look at me with that mischievous, bright, gap-tooth smile? My heart flutters with the thought of finding out. So tonight I'm going to come clean and tell her the truth. Even if she thinks I'm creepy for wanting to date my almost-step-sister.

But in my opinion, almost doesn't count.

"Hey, I'm pulling up now," Hen says when I answer the incoming call. "Where are you?"

"I'm waiting by the entrance. Come in through the Melrose end of Bernado. There's a spot in front."

"On it," she says.

I see the warm glow of her headlights heading in my direction a few seconds later, and relief floods my system. However, as soon as I go to meet her, some dickhead in a LED monstrosity of a truck pulls out of the alley and swoops into the space. His smug smile pisses me off when he spots Hen behind him, cussing up a storm. Yet the way he parked pisses me off more. He's not even facing the right direction. I have half a mind to try and get him towed.

"It's fine, Jaima," Hen calls as she pulls up next to me. "My homegirl lives a block over. I'll park at her house and walk down.

"Are you sure? I can get him moved," I counter.

"Jay, that's not very Christmas spirit of you," she giggles. "It's fine. I can use the steps anyway."

She pulls off before I can reply. Which is fine because I don't have much to say.

I'm still stuck on the fact that she gave me a nickname, because to my delusional, lesbian brain, this feels like a step in the right direction.

I wonder what kind of cereal she likes in the morning?

I end up having to wait for Hen inside after some creepy ass middle aged dad asks me if I'm selling it, and rather than ruin our night for pepper spraying a man, I choose peace.

If peace was watching the truck asshole win a ham for being the 100th attendee through the doors. After he cut Hen off.

While I prefer Pernil, something about watching an entitled white man taking something that would and should've gone to a woman disturbs my spirit.

So I do what anyone would do.

I wait until his drunk ass goes to the bathroom to steal his ham off the table.

It's too big for my Telfar, so I just tuck it under my arm and head to the car.

In perfect timing, Hen meets me at the door.

"Hey, are you- Wait, is that a ham?"

"Yeah, I'll explain it in a bit. But right now we need to

leave."

"Leave?" she asks as I pull her along. "Why?"

"Before that guy in the truck comes out of the bathroom."

"The guy that cut me off?" I nod and Hen quickly follows me to my coupe parked on the opposite side. Thank God for remote start, because by time I get the car in drive, Scammed and Dehammed is running outside after us.

"Hey! That bitch stole my ham!" he shouts."

It's payback, hoe!" I screech in reply as I flip him my middle finger. "Merry Christmas, bitch!"

All I hear is my tires screeching against the wet pavement as we rip away from the club and hop on the 101. I usually like the quiet, but I've gotten used to listening to music when me and Hen are together. She has amazing taste in neo+soul and R&B. Unfortunately she's screaming before I can ask her to connect her phone.

"Jaima! What the fuck was that? You stole that man's ham? I thought you were dressed as Scrooge as a joke, not a reenactment!"

I try my best not to laugh, but I can't help that small giggle that escapes when I notice Hen's dressed like an elf. From the jingle bell hat to her striped stockings. It's adorable despite her confused mean mug.

"First off, that was your ham. He stole your parking space. Really, it was reparations."

"Ok, fair. But what about the party? We can't really go back. I mean well we could. I'm strapped. But I don't wanna get into a shout-out over a ham. That's too much."

"Hen!? You have a gun?" I gasp.

"Jay, I'm a five-foot-four tattoo artist who started in

Compton. Of course I have a piece."

"You're right. My bad. But hold tight, I have a backup."

"Alright," she sighs. "But I get the AUX!"

"Thank goodness," I chuckle.

Thirty minutes later, we arrive at a lounge tucked away near the river. It's one of those spots that's bigger inside than it initially appears, and it's cozy without you having to worry about your knees touching the people at the table next to you. I order us two apple pie eggnogs before locating my favorite booth near the back. Closest to the painting of a Dahomey warrior. I take note of the sprig of mistletoe tied to the booth lamp as I help Hen with her jacket.

"This is pretty," Hen whispers. "It reminds me of an art gallery."

"The owner actually runs an art gallery a few blocks down. Reminisce is what it's called."

"I've seen that before. I keep telling myself to go in there."

"Maybe we can make a date out of it," I shrug.

"Oh," she gasps. "Like as friends?"

"No," I whisper as I inch closer. "Not as friends."

For a second I debate on how much to tell her, but I figure honesty might be my best and only shot. I want her to know everything. Even the ugly parts I try to stuff down and cover up.

"Hen, I hate Christmas," I start.

"Still? Damn it."

"No, just hear me out. I hate Christmas because my mom started to decline around this time twelve years ago, and that's all I can remember about the season most days. Knowing that she was in pain despite smiling and being cheerful for everyone else. So those feelings may remain for a few years, but despite that I really like spending it with you."

"Even after today's ham incident?"

"Especially after today's ham incident," I nod as I tuck an errant loc behind her ear. "It reminded me that new memories can lessen the pain of old ones."

"You wanna make new memories with me?" she whispers as we grow closer.

"Yeah, real bad. Even if it means giving up some of my suits for stretch knit."

I have another joke planned, but it gets lost between our lips meeting for a tender kiss. I can taste the shea butter lipgloss on Hen's skin, and the cinnamon from her last drink. It's so much sweeter than I dreamed it would be and the push and pull of our mouths easily disconnects me from this reality. Until a man interrupts.

"Wow, that's hot," he says through cracked lips and yellowing teeth.

I don't get angry often, but let me set the scene. Imagine waiting months to kiss someone. Dreaming of them, pining for them, hoping that they want you the way you want them, only for a random dirtbag to intrude on the most magical moment of your life.

It makes me crave violence.

I begin to launch the napkin holder at his creepy ass, but Hen stops me with a quiet request. "Help me with something in the bathroom?" she pleads. I begrudgingly follow her hand-in-hand to the two-stall ladies' room where silence awaits us. She's just looking at me expectantly and that's when I notice she's wearing a jumpsuit.

"Oh, do you need me to unzip you?"

"What?" she asks before I motion to the back of her garment.

"No Jaima, damnit. I need you to kiss me. Without some funky ass man potentially beating off to the memory of it later."

"Wow, you know just what to say," I chuckle.

"Yeah, now shut me up before I think of something else."

We fall back into a breathless rhythm. Hen's hands are tangling in my loosening curls as our pecks grow more urgent. She's covered in my lipstick and my face and neck is slick with the remnants of her beauty-store gloss. Nothing about this is neat and orderly like my usual dates, and the realization makes my heart race. I'm doing something right for once. I'm down on my knees before I can talk myself out of it. The cool tile serves as my only source of salvation from the heat between us as my fingers creep up her expansive thighs, admiring the dips and craters of Hen's glorious body.

"Is this ok?" I ask as my thumb traces the soft lace of her panties.

Her *yes* comes out as a needy, tender whine, and I let my greedy fingers slip underneath the fabric there and spread her lips.

"So wet," I groan. "You're so wet for me, mamas."

I stroke her stiff clit with gentle, slow measures, allowing her plenty of time to acclimate to the sensation. Hen happily spreads her legs, silently begging me to continue, and I oblige her. My middle and ring finger sinks into her tight entrance, pushing and pumping along to the rhythm of the jazz playing in the background while I work her bud. Her cries are quiet but demanding. She begs me not to stop and I don't. Not until we're both covered in a thin sheen of sweat and she's writhing against the sink in ecstasy. It's satisfying to see her soft like this.

Until she looks at me with renewed hunger in her eyes.

"Hen, wait," I plead as she pulls me onto my feet and pushes me against the wall. "There's something I really need to tell you."

She doesn't listen, she just drops to her knees and pulls those pretty, tattooed titties out of her suit. I'm sad to say that it's all it takes for her to distract me. Because the common sense doesn't return until she's already un-zipped my pants and slipped her fingers into the waist-band of my panties. She eagerly yanks the satin fabric down with her tongue between her lips, but what comes tumbling out isn't what she expects. I don't expect it either because I've long since perfected my tuck, but I also didn't think I'd be hard to the point of dizziness. So it's a shock to both of us when my dick plops out and smacks her square in the middle of her forehead.

"Um, I'm trans," I whisper nervously.

"Oh," she mumbles, with my tip still practically poking her in the temple. "I see."

"I'm sorry I didn't tell you. I didn't really expect you to lick it in the middle of the bathroom."

"Are you seriously fucking apologizing?" she hisses.

"Listen, you never know people's genital preferences. I usually like to have the talk beforehand. I didn't think I would make you cum in a lounge."

"Well, I don't have a genital preference. I like pretty girls. Do you like pretty girls?"

"Yes, very much."

"Ok, then we're fine. All cum goes down the same in my eyes."

It's not the appropriate moment to realize that I'm going to marry this woman, but it's the moment it happens nonetheless. Everything clicks in place for me. I can see the rest of my life in her big brown eyes, and it looks wonderful.

Then I see panic when we hear a knock at the door.

"Excuse me? Is anyone in there?" someone calls. "The door is locked."

Neither one of us says anything, we just scramble off the wall, tuck my dick back in my pants, and then unlock the door as we pretend to be working on Hen's zipper. The lady who was waiting looks at us with sympathy as Hen wiggles down into the fabric.

"Jumpsuits are so cute until you realize you have to pee," she sighs.

"Right?" Hen groans. "That's why they're a team effort."

"Mhm. That's the real reason us girls travel to the bathroom in packs. For sticky zippers."

We laugh as we wash our hands. She's so nice that I almost feel bad for blatantly lying, but that guilt dissolves when Hen closes out our tab and pulls me outside.

"Take me home?" she asks with a soft kiss.

"Of course," I nod.

Hen

I'm still upset that she apologized. What the fuck is that to apologize about? I have a bi flag tattooed on my ass! Clearly I don't give a fuck, and I'm pissed that she feared

I would. I'm also upset after finding out she's had a crush on me since last year. We could've been making out in her coupe months ago. Luckily for both of us, Jaima's sooo good at making amends.

"Fuck, fuck, fuck, baby fuck!" I screech.

If I had on nails, they'd all be broken by this point. She's been twirling her tongue in my cat for the last thirty minutes and there's nothing else for me to grip on to survive this ride. My body shakes with yet another release as she sucks my clit between two fingers. At this point I'm no longer moaning, I'm speaking in tongues. Yet no matter who or what I call on, she's not letting up.

"Jaima, time out. I need water," I whine.

She pops up from between my legs looking like a freshly glazed Krispy Kreme donut wearing nothing but an apologetic smile.

"Sorry. You taste so good that I got carried away. I can grab you a drink. Do you want a bottle or a glass?"

"Let's do both just to be safe," I groan.

I'm glad I gave Jaima the house tour before she slipped and fell between my thighs, because she returns with refreshments in record time. It's just how I like it too, chilled but not freezing, with just enough condensation on the glass to dampen my fingers. I'm ashamed at how fast I suck down the first cup, but it's been two years since my last encounter with another woman.

Big Mama is worn out.

"Still need a minute?" she asks while sweeping my hair out of my eyes.

"Yes," I pout. "I was scared my pussy would explode."

We fall back into the pillows with laughter echoing off the walls. Jaima's loose curls fan around us like a halo and for a second I imagine her in a white dress while wearing the same endearing smile. I like the way my life looks with her in it.

"Look what came," I whisper while reaching for the box on the nightstand.

I pass it to her so she can open it, but Jaima being Jaima has to read the shipping label first.

"Is this what I think it is?" she asks while slipping the jar out of the packing peanuts. "It is. Oh, yours turned out so pretty."

"Let's light it and see how it smells," I suggest.

Jaima is insistent on trimming the wick first, and I'm happy to let her rock as she cuts it down to the closest millimeter. Five minutes later the scent of decadent dark chocolate and sharp peppermint surrounds us like a warm hug. Despite the stolen ham chilling in my fridge, I'm in heaven.

"Can I admit something?" she asks, as we watch the shadow of the flame dance against the wall.

"Of course."

I expect her to tell me she had a pang of jealousy when she thought I was making my candle for a non-existent girlfriend, which I knew because she didn't hide it well at all. She taps her nails when she's irritated.

"I don't get the whole wax thing. Is it like a thrill seeking kink?"

"Oh, sweetness. No. It's a sensory thing. Did you ever dip your fingers in melted candle wax as a kid?"

"Mhm."

"Ok, good. Now imagine that sensation on erogenous zones."

"I'm trying, but to be honest you might've lost me again."

"That's fine, I can show you better than I can tell you. Pick a safe word."

Of course her safe word is Abacus. I have to admit it's a good one. Nobody accidentally says abacus in the middle of hunching. We're pressed together tight, hands tangled in each other's curls as our lips exchange the sweetest of silent promises. She probably doesn't know it yet, but I'm going to marry her.

First though, I'm gonna fuck her.

It pains me to separate from her, from the little whine that escapes her when I break our kiss, to the loss of the heat between us. However, I cope with the space by telling myself it's for the greater good. I want Jaima to have everything the world has to offer and more. Including pleasures both known and unimaginable.

I tip the candle over slightly, letting the warm, rich, brown wax drip between us in wide splatters.

"Oh, that's warm," she whimpers.

"Too much?"

"No, just unexpected."

"Ok, remember to use your safeword if it's too much, pretty girl."

I start again, and this time I get lost in the action. It looks like chocolate sauce staining our skin, sticky, sweet, and delectable. It rolls down the valleys of Jaima's breasts, onto her belly, and settles in the creases of her hips. That's when I realize I have to let some more wax melt, but waiting is half the fun. The stiff peaks of my nipples press into Jaima's, spreading the cooling wax onto our areolas with every teasing swipe. My mouth is back on hers, and this time I don't have to worry about stopping because she has the candle pouring handled. She takes my chin in her palm as she coats us with fresh wax, claiming my every breath and moan. I never know what's coming with her. She'll hold me with all her strength one minute, and then send me floating away with barely there caresses the next. Everything about her is overwhelming. Especially the familiar yet foreign pleasure aching in my core every time our bodies meet.

Wait.

Am I about to nut from nipple play?

"Jaima, wait," I cry. "I think I'm gonna cum."

"Cum for me, Hen. I need to know what it looks like when you cum on top of me, baby," she commands while fixing my hips to hers.

That voice of hers when she's in the mood is eventually going to be a problem, because it's really good at making me comply. I relax into the pleasure at her instruction. I finally let the hot, sticky, friction of the wax as it thickens and sets on our rubbing titties send me over the edge. Spots darken my vision at an alarming rate as I tumble off a cliff. It's a different kind of orgasm this time because it didn't come from my clit, but it's so strong that it knocks me over. I'm both amazed and slightly embarrassed at the startled cry that comes out of me when it happens. Until Jaima's shy smile reminds me that this is a first for both of us.

"I usually have a little more stamina than that," I laugh anxiously.

"I'm not judging," she cooes while rubbing my back. "I doubt I'll last longer than three minutes inside of you."

"Don't be modest."

"Please. I'm not modest, I'm realistic. You're soft, and warm, and you smell like toasted vanilla. I know I'm going to embarrass myself."

"Well then we'd be even. So do you wanna try anyway?" I giggle.

Jaima

My eyes are fixed on the little lightning bolt-shaped tuft of hair on Hen's mound as she rolls a condom down the curve of my dick. It's unexpected, like everything else today. Especially her room. It's not moody like I would expect for a famous tattoo artist. It's mounds of soft pink and fluffy fixtures. From her lamps to the shag rug trimming the floor, it's unbelievably cozy. If I wasn't pressing the points of my nails into my palm, I'd assume that I actually passed out at the resort from low sugar and this was all a fever dream. Now that I know it isn't though, I feel high. Like I'm floating outside of my body.

Or maybe even outside of my realm.

"You alright, love bug?" Hen asks.

"I'm alright. Just having a little trouble believing you're real."

"I'm real, Jaima. This is real," she cooes while holding my cheek. "We're gonna go slow. Ok?"

"Ok," I whimper.

Hen holds my face for a while longer before her hand

slips backs down between us, dragging my tip over her clit, through her lips, and down to her entrance. She hovers, allowing me time to come to terms with our impending union, before slowly sinking down. Watching my length disappear inside her pink palace has my entire body shaking even before she's fully seated, and it gets worse when she decides to call out my name.

"Jaima," she whimpers as her pussy flutters around me. "Why do you feel so good?"
My mouth opens but the only thing that comes out is a strangled moan.
Yeah I can't entertain a conversation with her right now, I'm barely remembering to breathe. So to keep her from asking questions that I don't have an answer to, I fold her lips into mine. She still tastes like cinnamon, funny enough. I'm starting to think that may just be her natural taste. Earthy, sweet, and slightly spicy. Just like the rest of her.

Somehow the thoughts of our "not dates" are grounding me through all our tumultuous movement.
I hate to admit it, but she really did make this holiday season bearable for me. Lately all I can remember about Christmas is how good Hen looked in her ugly tattoo sweaters, how pretty the snow in Big Bear is, and the bridge to This Christmas by Donny Hathaway. It's extended my pathetic stamina up from three minutes to six and a half.
Just as long as I don't think about her ass as it bounces up and down in my lap. It's so much ass.
Under these circumstances, it's almost too much ass.

"You're sweating," she says while cupping my left tit.

"I'm struggling," I whimper. "I'm almost at the end of pi."

"You can cum, Jay. You've been such a good girl, you deserve to cum."

"No, not yet," I pout as I mirror her caress.

"Do you want me to cum with you?"

"Yes please."

Hen smiles before leaning over to fetch something out of her nightstand. It's a small pink frog that vibrates, and it fits perfectly between her clit and labia.

"I like that you're a secret freak," I admit. "Cause how did you even find something like this?"

I was in the UK for a competition and I visited some of their stores. I also have a butterfly. Is it too weird?"

"No, but it's strong. We probably got about two more minutes," I moan.

"That's all I need," she whispers before slipping my nipple into her mouth.

Our conversation peters out as we regain our rhythm. Slow, deep, and hard. Like the motion of a mortar against smooth fufu.

She's wet, tight, and hot as she rocks against me. You can hear it in every single stroke. Wet, obscene, suction that leaves nothing to the imagination. If the Lord is truly always watching, I know he'd have to cover his ears right now. I love it though. It's confirmation that I make her feel good. So while I'm content listening to the sounds our bodies make, I know she needs more than that to reach the finish line.

"You feel so good, Hen," I moan as I nibble her ear. "I can tell you're close. Do you wanna cum with me? It would be so much fun if you did."

"Jaima, please," she hisses.

It's not a no, so I wet my thumb in the mess she's made before easing it in her tight ass. Suddenly we're frantic, with her chasing the inevitable end and me chasing her. I grip the sheets so hard that I worry they may have ripped but I'm trying to ground myself. I'm trying not to become absolutely obsessed with the woman on top of me. I'm trying not to lose my soul in her velvety brown eyes. I'm trying not to picture her in a white dress and a long veil, with all her tattoos on display as she walks down a sandy aisle to become my wife. However once Hen calls out my name at the height of her summit, I realize that the attempt to resist is useless. We spiral together, hand in hand, chest to chest. Our breathing deepens as we crumble into pieces, and it syncs as we come to a stop. Restoring each other with gentle touches, grateful, heaving sighs, and sweet nothings.

"Stay the night?" she pleads, still breathless and exhausted.

"I'm not going anywhere," I say as I pull the blankets over our cooling bodies. I omit that I mean generally and not just for the night. We'll get to that eventually.

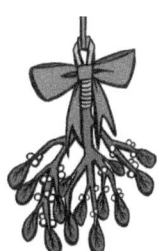

7
THE GAY AGENDA

Hen

It's Friday, and we're supposed to be doing a movie marathon while binging holiday snacks, but Jaima's in my bed after a long night. For a while I wondered if I drank too much and imagined everything, but no. Her endless legs are really sprawled across the wrinkled sheets as she rests her head on my shoulder, snoring her little cartoon mouse snore. If I could take an aerial snapshot of this moment and frame it, I would. Everything about this morning is perfect. It's exactly what society tells little girls they can expect in romance through princess movies and teen rebellion cinema. Minus some trash ass man sweating up my sheets.

I pick up my phone to check the time and order us some breakfast, but Arnetta's timing is nothing if not divine. My phone starts vibrating as soon as it's hovering above my face and in an effort not to wake Jaima by having it sound off in her ear, I accidentally drop it on my face and split my lip.

"Shit, that fucking hurt," I hiss.

Unfortunately that startles Jay and she sits straight up like someone electrocuted her. I start to tell her it's fine and that she can go back to sleep, but my phone rings again. It seems angry this time. Like a scorching voicemail awaits me if I don't answer. This woman is relentless, but I guess it's the wedding stress.

"Hi, Mama. Good morning," I huff.

"Henny, are you still sleeping? Girl, you must've had a late night session."

Yeah, I had a session alright. Jaima blushes beside me as she tries to smooth her thick curls back into a somewhat sleek ponytail. She's moving too fast though, so her rubberband breaks. Which results in her having a silent temper tantrum until I move to do it for her.

"Uh, something like that," I chuckle nervously as I brush Jaima's hair back into a bun. "What's up?"

"I didn't mean to wake you up, but have you heard from Jaima? We know you two were supposed to be hanging out later today, but she was supposed to meet James for coffee this morning at 9 and he can't get ahold of her."

"Fuck! What time is it!?" she gasps as I snap the scrunchy in place.

I pinch my eyes shut, hoping and praying Mama won't say anything about the unladylike cursing or recognize the voice of the perpetrator. I beg God. I promise to go to church this year. At least on Christmas and Easter.

However my prayers go unanswered.

"Henrietta, do you have a lady over? Did I interrupt something?"

Mostly unanswered. At least she doesn't recognize it's Jaima. So I guess I'm on the hook for Easter.

"Um, no. We're just talking about tattoos and stuff. Cereal, breakfast. Can I call you back later? I'll try to get in touch with Jaima in a second."

"Mhm, yeah that's fine," Mama says while sucking her teeth. "Tell your lil friend I said hello."

"Yeah, I'm not gonna do that. Talk soon though, lady."

I hang up with an exaggerated groan. That was not the morning of post-hunching bliss I was hoping for.

"What, I can't tell your mom hi?" Jaima teases as she sits down fresh glasses of water.

I down the whole cup before addressing her scandalous little question. I'm dehydrated from nutting out my soul, and I feel extra thirsty watching her stretch her arms over her head.

"Not wrapped in my sheets and smelling like my pussy, you can't."

"Are you ashamed of me?"

"No, I'm ashamed of myself. She told me to get to know you, not corrupt you."

"You did get to know me, just a little more... Intimately."

"You got jokes this morning."

"Yeah, maybe even tomorrow morning too."

As I trace all of my hopes and affections into the lines of Jaima's open palm, a question populates in my mind. I've had my fair share of quick fucks, but this doesn't feel like those did. It feels like something that can change the trajectory of my life.

"Do you like me for real or is this just sex?" I ask her in a small voice.

"Funny, I was about to ask you the same thing," she whispers. "People usually leave by now."

We stare at each other for a while, eyes watering from the pain of being vulnerable before twelve noon. Some neurotic part of me starts to wonder if this would be easier with a man. Because they would've just admitted that they just thought my ass was fat and dipped. Instead Jaima says,

"I think about you constantly. Even when I'm asleep, but especially when I'm awake. I want you to be my girlfriend if you want me. I don't want you to leave."

"Duh. Of course I want you," I sob.

We fall into each other's arms with soft laughter. It's peaceful again as we stretch out together. Not heavy or loaded with tension of what's to come. I start to relax into my girlfriend and drift back asleep.

But then her phone rings and my eyes pop open.

It's James.

"Listen, I meant what I said. But we cannot tell our parents right now," she groans as she leaves the bed.

Fortunately we're on the same page. They're too high strung for us to throw anything new into the mix now. We need to get them married first.

"I agree. Let's give it a month."

"A month is good. I can get a reservation at that one brunch spot your mom likes. We can break the news in a public setting."

"Yolk and Yonder?"

"Yes. They'll have red velvet pancakes for Valentine's day."

"Ooh, I do love a good red velvet."

"I know. It's one of my favorite things about you," she says with a soft smile. "Ok. I have to go. But I'll send a Muver for your car and I'll be back at four for movies."

"Ok, be safe. See you soon," I say as I peck her.

"See you soon. Let me know if you wanna play, *my step-sister is stuck in the dryer*, later."

"Jaima, get out."

"Ugh, fine. Have a good day, gorgeous."

"You too, beauty."

Jaima

"Where you coming from, girl?" Daddy shouts.

I originally told him I was coming from home. Which was true because I desperately needed a shower after dealing with Hen all night. However, for some reason he refuses to believe me. So I scramble off ChowNow before he sees that I sent Hen breakfast. Not because I think he knows where she lives since he still texts me every few months and asks for my address of seven years, but because that will only lead to more questions that I can't answer right now. Namely, the question of potential grandchildren. Which is crazy because I barely have time for a cat right now.

"Apologies, Sir. I overslept this morning," I say.

"I can see that," he chuckles as he sits beside me. "I ain't seen you without makeup in years. God, you look like Mila. Got her freckles and everything. My genes never stood a chance. I'm just glad you kept my name when you transitioned."

"Hush you," I laugh with soft tears. "Before I go back and change it to Sienna or something."

"Oh, please. You can keep them empty threats. Sienna is a name for a horse and you know it," he chides as he squeezes my shoulder.

"What's got you so emotional lately? Hm? Is it Hen and her Christmas thing? You've been a lot more relaxed since you started hanging out with her. I knew she'd be good for you."

"What do you mean?"

"Well, y'all are opposites. You're all proper and prim and she's chaos, but good chaos. I figured she'll teach you how to unwind, and you'll keep her upright. Like sisters."

Actually, like wives, but I won't tell him that now.

"Hm."

"Mhm. Maybe she can even help you get a date."

"And this line of conversation is officially closing. Thank you. Let's get some food and talk about the rehearsal."

I can save face through a lot of things, but a potential fake date isn't one of them. I was about to implode when I thought Hen had a girlfriend.

"Fine, but I'm still holding my breath for my grandbabies. So just keep that in mind."

"Ok," I sigh.

The day creeps by. Daddy and I only spend an hour together because he's taken a page out of Hen's book by planning a quick weekend getaway for Arnetta. It's a nice catch-up that I'd normally find refreshing during my busy weeks. But today all it does is make me miss Hen more. She's at the shop doing a quick touch-up on a healed piece before our movie date. Normally I'd have plenty of shit to do to fill the time, but today I decide to take it easy and go visit my mom.

The flower shop on Rose Hills still has daisies by the time I get to Whittier, so I grab a dozen of the sunny yellow ones she loved so much and bring them with me. As I examine the petals, I realize they're the same daisies Hen has tattooed on her arms and legs. It's funny how life decides to take and give. Even if you don't laugh when it first happens.

It's a long, winding road to get to the plot of land she's buried on with my grandparents, and I drive it slowly, appreciating the sound of the gravel under my tires, and letting that good ancestral energy wash over me before I get out of the car. Her grave is clean, and I recognize Arnetta's handwriting on the card laying at her headstone. The ink is looped in a series of heartfelt thank you's, and as I sit on the patch of grass covering her casket, I once again feel grateful that Daddy met her.

"Hey, mommy," I say quietly as I trace her name and birthdate. "I miss you."
She used to love yap sessions when she was alive. I doubt anything has changed in death, so I spend at least an hour getting her all caught up on my life, including the

new thing between me and Hen. I have a feeling she'd be looking at me with a smirk if she could, all while telling me she knew that I'd fall for Hen eventually. I talk to her until the sky darkens with impending rain, and just as I pick myself up to head home, my phone rings.

"Hey, I finished a little early. Do you wanna meet me at Sprouts so we can grab some lunch before we get started?"

"I'd love to."

Hen

"Ok, these are comfy," Jaima sighs. "I still feel like I need some support though."

We're in matching Christmas pjs that I bought weeks ago, two days before I asked Jaima out to lunch the first time. I didn't have a rhyme or reason for the purchase at the time besides the upside down candy cane resembling a J, but I now realize that my subconscious knew what that lunch invite was leading up to. She looks so cute in her fuzzy plaid set that I want to take a picture and frame it. Unfortunately she's so used to structure that she's frowning.

"Here, I got your support," I say as I slide behind her and hoist her titties up in my hands. "Now what do you wanna watch first?"

"We're gonna be watching Wet Ebony Tribbing 5 if you don't let go of me," she growls.

"Let's start with something to take the edge off," I suggest with a giggle. "How about Last Holiday?"

"Oh, I love anything with Dana."

We watch Queen Latifah with a healthy dose of awe and nostalgia for two hours, sharing popcorn and commentary as necessary, IE when LL Cool J pops up on screen. Listen, I can respect the man as a Y2k heart throb, but I can't picture him as anyone's love interest after that song he did with J-Lo. "

Ugh, I forgot how much I used to love this movie," Jaima sighs as the credits roll.

"Me too," I nod. "Before the phatphobia ruined it."

"Oh my God. Diet culture was so bad. You know what else I can't watch as an adult? Moesha."

"Oooh her daddy was nervewracking as a motherfucker. I also can't do Love And Basketball anymore."

"What? You don't wanna play for my hand in marriage while my fiancee sleeps peacefully, weeks away from our wedding?"

"You gonna dunk on me too?"

"I got to," she chuckles. "It builds character."

We go into the next movie with cups of steaming cocoa, topped with fat, gooey strawberry marshmallows that Jaima bought while she was out at lunch. It's rich and delicious after all that salty popcorn, but also nostalgic with the cool rain pounding against the window. I finish my mug ten minutes into the movie and the heat from the drink settles in my chest and belly, encouraging me to sink into Jaima's side. The bed creaks a few times as I figure out the best position for watching TV while propped up on a pair of tig ole bitties. I eventually find that it's tucked under her chin, my ear to her heart as she holds me close.

On screen we watch Terrence Howard share a blunt with Monica Calhoun to ease her pain.It's supposed to be a quiet moment of comedic relief between them, but instead of laughing like I always do when he bursts through the doors, I erupt into tears.

"Hey, hey. What's up?" Jaima asks while blotting my wet face.

"Sorry, it's just. He reminds me so much of my dad. He was always doing stuff like that," I say with a choking sob. "I know it's kinda silly, but I just miss him so much."

"No, don't apologize, sweetness. That's the whole point of life. To love and remember the ones we lost."

"Doesn't it ever make you scared? Love I mean? To realize that one day you'll be sitting alone with all the memories?"

"Of course it makes me scared," she laughs as tears streak her cheeks. "But the fear isn't worth giving up moments like this. I'll always cherish the memory of how it felt to hold you for the first time, even when we're old, gray, and bedridden. Even if you have to leave first."

"I'm really starting to hate sappy Christmas movies," I chuckle as I bury myself in the warmth of Jaima's embrace.

"Really? That's weird because I was just starting to love them."

I relax into the soft peck placed on my temple, letting the pain of a distant memory ebb into gratitude for life, love, and in this particular situation, even loss. I love my dad, but without his death, I would have never met James and eventually Jaima.

"Is it too soon to say I love you?" I whisper softly.

"Probably, but we're gay. You basically proposed when you got me custom skates."

"Oh please. When I propose, you'll know."

"Wait, you're proposing?"

"Yes duh. Because I obviously love you and eventually I'll need you to be my wife."

"Well I love you too, and I can't wait to be your eventual wife."

"You wanna get married on Christmas too?" I tease as we meet for a kiss.

"Henny, please don't push it. It's a miracle I didn't break out in hives when we hung the mistletoe."

"Ok, Scrooge. I won't push it. One Christmas wedding is more than enough for this lifetime."

"Ugh. You can say that again."

8
LET'S GET MARRIED

Jaima

"You are being paid quadruple your regular rate for a 300 person party. If you'd like your dad to keep the signing bonus and the contract with Corla, I don't want to see a single sprig of dill out of line!" I hiss.

I can tell he wants to call me a bitch, but he holds it when his dad comes around the corner.

Bless Hen for finding us a caterer so short notice, but the owner's son is pissing me off. We made triple sure to inform them about Hen's dairy allergy just for me to see him flinging cheese around this bitch willy nilly. The schedule is already tight. The last thing we need is for the daughter of the bride to be glued to a toilet during the cocktail hour and reception.

"Fix that row of chairs, please," I moan as I pass the great hall.

It's crooked as hell and that pisses me off on its own. But since watching every Christmas movie under the sun with Hen, I can also confidently say that they also look like young Tom Cruise's gangly teeth. Honestly Arnetta picked the perfect venue. Dorado Station is a vision with its grand chandeliers, molded ceilings, and hand paint-ed murals adorning the walls. It's especially captivating when it's all dressed up for winter. However, no one can dedicate their focus to all those beautiful things due to the half-assed seating arrangements!

"Hey, there you are," Hen exclaims jubilantly. "I've been looking for you. Makeup is about to start."

This is the moment that makes me 100% certain that God is a woman. Because she had to create Henrietta Brighton in her image. Everything about her is divine. From her locs that were coiled into a perfect ponytail on top of her head, resembling a blooming lotus. To her soft tummy, tempting me through layers of cream satin and glittery mesh. To her toes peeking through her heels, showing me just a hint of baby pink polish.

It makes me wanna lick them.

Holy shit, am I into feet? My dad's wedding day is a crazy time to find out I'm into feet.

"You aight? You look stressed."

"I am," I sigh.

I leave out the fact that she's raising my blood pressure

more than anything else happening here. It's just not fair for her to be this beautiful at 10AM.

"Well, we got fifteen minutes before we're due upstairs. You wanna kiss a little?"

My eyes fall to her plump lips, glistening with a light sheen of gloss, and then to her ass, looking just like a Christmas ham, brown sugar glaze included.

"Sure we can kiss," I say while pulling her along to an empty dressing room. "Let me just take one of these…"

"Oh, fuck!" Hen whimpers as her thighs vibrate with pleasure. "Merry Christmas to me."

She's about to melt into the chair, but I keep licking her
like a cup of shaved ice because she tastes sweet, and
because a very primal part of my brain realizes that she's
probably ovulating. I can't fuck her because while we both
want kids, it's too soon. I don't like being unprepared for
big life changes and I'll be damned if I give that man a
grandchild in nine months. But I can eat her pretty pussy
until she passes out or the others start looking for us.

You know, whichever happens first.

I curl my fingers against her walls, encouraging her to
ride my palm while I suck her cute, swollen clit. She's
doing such a good job of relieving my stress with her soft
moans and quiet pleading. Especially when she nuts on
my face. Gooey isn't the word. It's a thousand times better
than the gel shit you can get at the Marriot.

"Good girl, Henny," I coo as I rub her leaking cooch.
"That's a big cummie, mamas."

"Don't look so satisfied," she growls back. "I'm gonna fuck
the shit out of you later."

"Ohh, are you gonna fuck me?" I tease as I continue to
pump her. "Are you gonna whip out the big cactus strap
and fuck me in the ass?"

"Until you scream my name."

"Hm, that's nice. A brat with an attitude. Now hush up all
that bitching and start moaning so we can go get pretty."

I press my flattened palm to the bottom of Hen's belly and
she does just that, making me grateful that I decided to
grab a napkin before we came in here. Otherwise I would
look like I got caught in the rain.

"Don't forget to wash up before you head upstairs," Hen huffs as she sinks onto the floor.

She looks wonderfully sated and almost boneless. She probably won't even cuss her Aunt Mary out today.

"I won't," I nod. "I know I can't smell like I've been in it during the ceremony, but maybe during the reception..."

"Jaima," Hen chides. "Save it for home. Or else I'm gonna ruin your tuck and this furniture."

"Don't tempt me," I say as she pulls me down for a quick peck. "I'm already wet."

"See you upstairs," she sighs while sweeping my edges back in place.

"See you upstairs."

Hen

"How do I look?" Mama asks.

She spins around like a ballet dancer, letting the fabric of her gown do its job at displaying her slow, graceful movements. The gown is tailored to perfection because Jaima made sure there wasn't a stitch of lace out of line, not one single errant thread. From her cropped curls to her perfectly rounded nails, and her bright, Christmas red painted smile, everything about her looks ethereal. So of course I break out in tears the moment our eyes meet.

"Oh, mommy," I sob as I pull her in for a hug. "You look so beautiful."

I'm trying my best not to crease either of our faces or wrinkle the dresses, but resisting the urge to dramatically faint is difficult. It took a long time for my mother to get her glow back, and this is the brightest I've ever seen her.

"Thank you baby, and so do you. I must say this dress looks phenomenal on you."

"It was Jaima," I sniffle.

"I figured," Mama giggled. "She was texting somebody about making you a dress before we even left the shop."

"Ugh, I hate how thoughtful she is."

"Speaking of Jaima. Where is she? It's almost time."

Honestly?

Probably somewhere swishing some mouth wash so she didn't smell like cooter during the vowels. We split up after makeup so she could check on catering and I could set the DJ up. I know she was having issues with Caleb, Kenny's son, but I didn't think it would take her long to threaten him into submission.

"I'm here!" she groans. "I just had to grab something from downstairs, and- Oh, Arnetta. You look absolutely gorgeous."

Mama starts tearing up again as she reaches for Jaima, who seems to be fighting the urge to hug her back.

"I'm not gonna squeeze you because I would absolutely wrinkle your dress," she sniffles. "But I want you to know that I love you and I'm really glad you're marrying my dad. Also, I brought you this."

Jaima extends her hand forward to offer Mama a silver tennis bracelet with sparkling sapphires. We all audibly gasp when it catches the early afternoon sunlight.

"I saw your Mom's wedding photos and I noticed she had something similar for her something blue. So I thought you might like this since she couldn't physically attend this wedding."

Me and Aunt Mary rush forward with tissues to catch the rainstorm of Mama's tears. If I wasn't dead-set on marrying Jaima before, I definitely am now. This is exactly who want to be the mother of my children. Ham-stealing, Christmas aversion and all.

"Ok, everybody dry those tears and put on your best smile!" the planner instructs. "It's showtime ladies."

I'll tell you one thing, the venue wasn't lying about this hall being great. We can see the sunlight pouring in from the lancet windows halfway down the hall. It casts a golden halo on everything and everyone, including the woman I love, as she floats down the aisle with her groomsman to the sweet soliloquy of harpsong. I fall in line behind her, my steps slowing as I imagine her in James' place, waiting on me with the same nervous smile. The white definitely doesn't help with my wedding psychosis, and while I know it's too soon, I also know that this is inevitable for us.

I'm gonna marry Jaima Hines.

Eventually.

We had the privilege of seeing her before everyone else, but we still hold our breath when the grand doors are pulled open to reveal Mama, looking like heaven on Earth in her pink gown. Jaima is crying before she can even make it halfway, and despite not wanting to blow our cover, I can't help but to reach up and blot her tears.

"They look so happy," she whispers.

"They do."

"I love them.

"Me too," I nod.

Mama settles beside James and her smile is just as dazzling and intoxicating as his while the preacher begins the ceremony. We hear about their triumphs, their tribulations, and how love was the thing that conquered all of that. We laugh, we cry, and at 3:56PM on a rainy Tuesday afternoon, we celebrate. Just as Mama says I do, and right when James prematurely kisses her as his wife. I cheer loudly as they jog down the aisle, hand in hand as Mr. and Mrs. Brighton. Even though Jaima is now officially my stepsister, today is-

Jaima

"Today was perfect," I say as I spin Hen around.

The band is playing the instrumentals to Silent Night while we float around on the dance floor with woozy little smiles, courtesy of all the leftover eggnog. We're definitely going to be hung over tomorrow, but it's fine because we're still able to dance now. I don't know how Hen does it, but she's been in heels for hours and she still looks radiant and refreshed. Meanwhile I look dog-tired. Haggard even. I was so worried about something going wrong that I could barely sleep last night. Now though I'm relaxed, because our parents are married, people are going home, and everything went off without a hitch. Even the tree in the courtyard with guest ornaments is perfection. Probably because it was Hen's idea.

"It was a good day even though it's Christmas?" Hen giggles.

"Especially because it's Christmas. You look really pretty under all the lights."

"You always look really pretty. Especially now with your curly little edges."

"You're just saying that cause you wanna get in my panties."

"Oh, I'm gonna get in those regardless. I just thought you should know that you're drop dead gorgeous and I'm really happy that you're my girlfriend... Slash stepsister."

I feel myself blushing under the soft yellow glow from the string lights and I have to remind myself not to kiss Hen's pouty little lip. Which is a first because I normally can't stand PDA, but not when it comes to her sentimental ass. I want everything with her. Wet, nasty kisses in front of church aunties and all.

"Are you ready to get out of here?"

"Absolutely. There is no fried food here and I need something to soak up this liquor."

"On it, we'll order fries in the Muver."

Hen

We were so desperate to get out of our clothes once we got home that we didn't stop to think about the consequences. As the old adage goes, two baddies with fat asses and pretty titties walked into a room together... Of course Jaima kissed every inch of my exposed skin as soon as I stepped out of my gown, and what was I supposed to do? I had to thank her for the dress. It fit like an absolute glove and we both knew it was custom couture. So it was only fair for me to drop to my knees and take her in my mouth. One thing led to another and now we're halfway through a new bottle of lube with A Jaguar Christmas playing in the background. Yeah the fries and tenders are cold on the kitchen table, but I'm popping them hoes in the air fryer just as soon as we get done.

"Damn, Vixen. Just like that, baby," I whine.
As a tattoo artist, I can confidently say that arts and crafts remain my favorite way to unwind.
Especially with other women.
"I cannot believe you talked me into this," Jaima moans, sending her reindeer antlers jingling.
"The sex or the roleplay?"
"The roleplay, Santa baby."
I give my best ho-ho-Oh before another release takes me. The tingling from warm peppermint wax being poured on my nipples is what does me in this time. But the sight of Jaima's fat ass swallowing a purple crystal dildo definitely doesn't help. She didn't think scissoring was possible with her dick and all, but really it just added to the fun. Especially when I pulled out the double dildo.

"You're lucky your shit is so fat," she cries as we gyrate together. "Fuck, Henny. It's so good."
Her head tips between her shoulders so her lungs can release a sinfully ragged moan. The fluid motion of our hips is driving us deeper into the cyclone of pleasure, one that's inescapable and destined to end in destruction. I didn't know Jaima had a short refractory period until about two weeks ago, and by then the wet blankets were already sold out for the holidays. Unfortunately I'm too horny to give a fuck about putting a towel down, so these sheets will have to be burned.

"You're my favorite reindeer, I always have a good ride with you," I tease while slipping my thumb into her wet mouth.

She sucks it so good that I damn near blackout from the force of my orgasm. I feel the release everywhere, from my stretched pussy, and my full ass, to the tip of my clit that Jaima's relentlessly teasing with a sucker.

"I'm sorry, Henny," she whines. "That one was strong. I can't hold it."

"Don't hold it, Jay. You've been nice all year. Cum all up in your pussy, pretty mamas. Fill me up."

"I'm about to be really naughty," she moans as we roll into Amazon.

This is the moment where I thank God for birth control. Because while I'm fucking Jaima in two places and making a mess everywhere, all I can think about is how good her load is about to feel inside of me. Silky skin glides against silky skin. I relish in the safety of Jaima's softness as we fall off a steep cliff together, hand-in-hand. It's loud, it's messy, and it's probably one of the best nuts of my life. So I'll happily write Jaima's neighbor an apology card in the morning when she gives us a concerned side-eye at the mailbox. We won't be stopping any time soon anyway.

"I can't wait until you get me pregnant for real," I pout.

"Oh my God, Hen. That's an insane thing to say while I'm actively cumming in you."

"I know," I chuckle. "But I mean it."

"It's fine. I can't wait either," Jaima admits with a sentimental sigh. "This was the best Christmas ever, and I know it'll be even better when we're moms."

"Do you really mean it?"

"Of course I mean it. I can't wait to have bab-"

"No, not that. Of course you wanna put a baby in me. I'm talking about the Christmas thing."

"Yes, Hen. I really mean it. I had a great Christmas with you. Newly minted step-sisterhood and all."

"Ugh, stop reminding me about that," I groan.

"Nope! You're your sister's keeper," she cackles while kissing me. "And I can't wait to tell everyone."

EPILOGUE
2 months later

Jaima

"Ooh, they have crawfish benedict," Arnetta sighs. "That sounds lovely."

This is their first week back after a long honeymoon in Lesotho. They kept us updated every other day with tons of pictures and amazing videos of the land and people, but I have to admit that getting to hug them in person is better. I'm glad they're home. Even if they're back to calling us at the ass crack of dawn.

"What was the food like?" Hen asks.

"There was a lot of stew," Daddy sighs in anguish. I know he was struggling because he can't stand soup

"But I'll tell you one thing, they got the bread game on lock. I ate so much damn bread while we were there."

"Ugh, I love bread," Hen replies while sipping a bit of my coffee. "Me and Jaima went to that new Korean bakery the other day and I got like six scallion rolls."

"Oh those were good," I agree. "Especially with the chili eggs."

Our parents leer at us with equal parts curiosity and skepticism as we rehash the story of blowing $100 on bakery bread. I can tell James is already building a timeline in his head. He's probably trying to figure out if the workshop was the beginning or the thick of it.

"Y'all sure have been spending a lot of time together," Arnetta says, while peeping over her glasses.

There was no denying it, every time they called one of us, they talked to both of us. I was sure that's when the suspicion started.

"Actually that's what we wanted to talk to you about," I say.

The parents give each other another conspiring glance before turning their attention back to us. It makes me squirm. What do they know? Do they have concerns already? I've been dating Hen for two and a half months and I've never been so sure of anything, but right now I need a Xanax if I'm going to convince them to be sure of us too.

"We're dating," Hen says proudly while taking my hand. The action steadies my anxiety, and I'm able to nod in agreement while Daddy stares into my soul. The interrogation is about to start any second now. I can feel it.

"Henrietta," he sighs while switching focus. "You know family is important to us. Jaima wants to be a mother eventually. How do you feel about that?"

"Me and Jay actually talked about that really early on. I also want kids and we'll probably start–"

"Oh my God! Y'all are trying for a baby!?" Arnetta hollers. Half the restaurant turns to look at our table, and I almost dissolve into the booth. Our parents are now up out of their seats, dancing in the aisle. This is too much commotion for Tuesday brunch. You would think they just won the lottery.

"What? No!" Hen fusses. "Mama, I said we're starting the planning process. We want to get married first then it'll probably take us about a year to conceive."

As usual, they hear nothing but what they want to hear.

"James, did you hear that? We're gonna be grandparents, baby!"

"In two to three years," I interject.

"I knew it!" Daddy shouts. "Jaima was looking all lovelorn at the wedding. I told you."

"You did say it," Arnetta nods with a sly smile. "It's a Christmas miracle, Daddy Brown."

That's the perfect moment for me to notice James has on a Charlie Brown sweater. Then I remember that Hen loves roleplay and that kinks are theorized to be hereditary.

"Ew," me and Hen mumble simultaneously.

Our parents ignore us and continue to throw out baby names and proposed configurations for where our future child would sleep in their house. You would think we just announced a pregnancy. Hell, the restaurant staff definitely does.

"Don't you bring that over here," I hiss as a waitress tries to tip toe over with a congratulatory cupcake.

It's a sweet gesture, but we do not need to egg them on. I'd like to leave here without being sent a fertility tracker.

"So I take it you aren't mad?" Hen sighs while pinching the bridge of her nose.

"Mad?" Daddy chuckles. "About what? It's clear that you love each other. Jaima, I haven't seen you smile in public since you were a literal child. And Hen, you look much less uncomfortable with people's stares. This is all we wanted for y'all. To love and be loved."

"Oh, thank goodness. Jaima was worried you'd freak out about the whole stepsister thing."

"I mean that will be a little weird to some people," Daddy concedes. "But I finally understand that show Uncle Grandpa. Wait, can that be my name? Uncle-pa?"

"Absolutely not," I wave. "I will send you a pre-approved list."

"I'm gonna be Glamma," Arnetta sighs wistfully.

Then her and Daddy are back to ignoring us and talking about baby names.

"Well this went about as well as I expected it to," Hen giggles while stealing a get off my plate. "A public setting did not help."

"Not at all. The actual pregnancy announcement needs to be contained."

"I agree. Maybe a dinner party. Or a family vacation."

"Oh I like the idea of a family vacation. Me, you, sand, and-"

"Unlimited shrimp tacos."

"Yes, lovely," I giggle as I kiss her forehead. "Unlimited shrimp tacos. Maybe we can do that on our next Group Trip.

"I'd like that a lot, Jay," she cooes. "A whole lot."

ARIA DAZE

The end

THANK YOU!

I just wanted to take a moment to say thank you. I'm running up on my three year publishing anniversary and wow, what a way we have come. From conquering big wide knowledge gaps, to building ARC teams, and even my first signing event, y'all have held me down. Thank you so so much for all the love and support. I really could not ask for a better literary community, and as always, I look forward to catching you at the next book!

P.S.

If you liked this book, please consider leaving me a review. It helps others in the community discover my work!

ARCHED: SNEAK PEEK
(Content Warning! Dark Romance.)

L angston came into two new cases on Friday. One was transferred over from a previous physician who deemed it unsolvable, and one was a maelstrom of diagnoses that conflicted and overlapped. It seemed Zora was punishing him for pursuing her. Seeing such convoluted cases before the weekend would normally piss him off, but now it only fueled his lust further. Zora did yoga twice a week. Langston was sure she was spry enough for her legs to touch the headboard in missionary, and he couldn't wait to see it up close and personal.

He carefully worked through the patient notes and past medical histories, staying thorough yet quick while juggling his after-work thoughts. He wanted to wrap up and get to the weekend. Zora was likely home relaxing, and he had already declined dinner with his parents, letting them know he was stuck on call. While it was true, that wasn't the real reason for his absence. He had already made plans the week previous, and they were contingent on his ability to keep a secret and schedule.

They had similar educations, but Langston only had three degrees to Zora's four. Yet he arrogantly believed his to be more important. What good was her degree in communications when he had an electrical and computer engineering minor to override her lock? She wasn't going to communicate her way out of forced entry. There was nothing Zora had said yet that convinced him to leave her alone, and he was doubtful that would change.

Langston slowly opened the door to a clean living room. Everything was put away neatly, and she'd even managed to get the stain out the couch. He expected a bit of fanfare considering he was there unannounced, but as he got comfortable, he heard her shower running. She had probably just started to unwind from her day. Zora liked to work until her brain went numb. Clocking out didn't mean much to her overworking ass, but that was fine because Langston had a cure for that.

He went through her fridge first, looking for a suitable recovery meal before giving up and ordering groceries. Then he made his way to her room and spread out on her bed. Zora didn't believe in buying groceries, but she had good taste in furniture. Langston had never laid on a mattress so supportive, and he started to get a little jealous of her supposed fiance. How could a man be so spoiled and yet so incapable? He didn't cook, clean, out earn her, or even make her cum. Oson's shortcomings began to anger Langston, but his irritation quelled when he heard the small, soft footsteps of his prey.

"Hi," he snarled.
Zora looked up from her phone in a panic and it clattered to the floor when her grip tightened around her towel. Her heart pounded fiercely as she took in the sight in front of her. The long legs, the big arms, and the menacing grin that sparkled from the trickling sunlight. Langston Ude was lying naked on her bed.

"How did you get in here!?" Zora shouted.
Langston yawned like he was bored, crossed his arms behind his head, and flashed her a soft grin before answering honestly,
"I hijacked your lock."
Zora's heart shot up to her throat. She didn't know whether to run, scream, or call someone, but Langston issued a warning before she could decide.
"I have a signal jammer running so you and I could talk. Or you could do the stupid thing and run, but when I catch you, which I will, there'll be no talking."

Langston beckoned her over with one crooked finger, and she mindlessly obeyed. He was trespassing, but he was also right. He'd catch her if she ran and then she wouldn't have a chance to talk her way out of this situation. Langston could be reasonable. She just needed to make a convincing enough argument.

However, when he pulled Zora into his lap he only gave her a few seconds before grasping her throat. He made sure that she couldn't talk without choking, then he started his speech.

"I don't like being ignored. You've had years to learn that, Zora. Yet you continuously break our rules and avoid me."

"I'm engaged to s..."

Langston lunged forward to interrupt her, yelling so loud that the furious vibrato shook the picture frames trimming the walls.

"I DON'T CARE!" he roared.

He tightened his grip just slightly, making Zora dizzy and docile as he continued.

"I wanna fuck you, and you're gonna let me, or I'm gonna tell yo square-ass fiance that you came all over my dick two weeks ago."

The memory made her pussy act out. It was terrible timing, but the man knew how to make her wet. Still, she saw a way out. She just had to prevent herself from riling him further. Zora nervously looked down to the lubrication pooling in Langston's lap, making sure to avoid his demanding gaze.

"What if I say no?" she asked softly.

"What if you say no?" Langston chuckled while jerking back in disbelief. "I'm not sure why you think that's an option. But if you say no, I'm going to tell everyone that you're an adulterous whore, report you for having a subordinate relationship, and I'll probably end up fucking you anyway. So you can make this easier on both of us by sitting on my face and letting me enjoy myself."

Unfortunately that answered all Zora's questions. So she busied herself by tracing the adinkra tattoo staining Langston's ribs while considering her options. She could have an orgasm. An orgasm that would make her question her beliefs, morals, and God himself. Or she could have her life ruined. Langston wasn't bluffing, and knowing him, he probably already hacked into her security cameras and saved the footage of her mistake.

"Do you have any other questions, Zora? Or do you understand?"

Zora managed a nod which granted her throat release from Langston's tight grip.

"Good girl," he growled. "Now come sit on my face."

Zora reluctantly climbed onto his shoulders and Langston brought her hips forward so her throbbing cunt rested against his lips.

"I fucking hate you," she hissed as he began to lick her.

"Good for you, Zo. Now shut up and let me eat."

Knowing exactly who she was, Langston forced two fingers into Zora's mouth to silence her, and once she was sufficiently gagged, the entire world begin to melt away.

About the Author

A ria is a die-hard romantic and her main goal is to always be drying her eyes from something sickly sweet. She has been dreaming up romance stories since she was seven years old, with the first one being a Toy Story fanfic. She's also a Neo-soul and R&B enthusiast who's forever got a song stuck in her head. You can find her looking for good food, reading, writing, or enjoying time with her family in her free time. She lives happily in Saint Louis, Missouri with her middle school sweetheart-turned-husband and their adorably chaotic son. Her dream is to one day write inclusive stories that center BIPOC full-time, but for now, she labors in fraud as a working stay-at-home mom.

ALSO BY ARIA

Glory
https://www.amazon.com/dp/B0D1YH9BNH

Burry The Hatchette
https://www.amazon.com/dp/B0CT34SSS4

Candy Corn Curses
https://www.amazon.com/dp/B0DJLQ3W14

Rudy Jones's New Year's Resolution
https://www.amazon.com/dp/B0CLMWNPQJ

From Kingston, With Love
https://www.amazon.com/dp/B0CPDFXY9P

Bloom
https://www.amazon.com/dp/B0C82QWN2F

Candid
https://www.amazon.com/dp/B0BZMZVZ47

Human Resources

https://www.amazon.com/dp/B0DMR5NY9X